THE STARS IN YOUR EYES

Cindy V. Estes

Contents

S tella was left in the forest as a child, if she wouldn't have been saved that night she wouldn't have survived. She was raised by the hands of werewolves, one which she also was.

Chapter 1

It was really cold. I was freezing even though I was wrapped in a blanket. I felt my eyes tear up, and I started to cry.

It was night and pitch black outside, besides the stars shining upon me. The moon too, but it was covered up by something. Or someone. Suddenly it got darker.

I heard more of them coming to join the creature on my left side. For some reason I felt calm now, with them watching me. They were in a circle around me, looking curiously at my face.

Around me there was a group of dogs. No, a group of wolves. But they were a bit bigger than normal wolves.

A brown one, who had sparkling green eyes, put its nose against my belly. I started to giggle. My little hand went up between the wolfs eyes feeling the soft fur of it. It looked at me with both confusion and friendliness in its eyes.

All of a sudden the wolves became men and women. All of them naked, putting on clothes they had carried in their mouths.

Five men and three women.

"I wonder who abandoned you here." A woman picked me up into her arms. Without knowing why, I felt safe. The warmth of her body stopped me from being cold.

"We need to take it with us." Looking over at him who spoke I saw that he had dark blue eyes and dark brown hair. The moon made his eyes glimmer.

"We can't just take someones baby from the woods," a woman protested. I could tell that she was angry. Not only by her voice, also by how she was standing. She had her hands clenched, like she was getting ready to punch someone.

"But it will not survive the night if we don't take it with us!" It was the woman holding me that spoke. She was angry, very angry. But the warmth coming from her did not stop warming me.

"We can come back tomorrow with it, and seek for the parents of it," the woman holding me said, her voice changing into a calm tone. I noticed that she had really dark hair with a pair of light green eyes.

Then I felt her moving. Really fast.

I woke up after the dream, opening my eyes slowky. I've had the same one for the past five nights now. It was a memory of the day I got rescued. The dream got longer and longer for each night. All the people in the dream was some the people that I knew of as my family, as my pack.

My real parents were never found, they told me. But I was still not sad, I had never met my real parents. At least I didn't have any memories of them. No one knew why, they found me when I was about one year old. Which means I had been with them for about a year, right? Why was every teeny tiny little memory gone then?

Many people thought that I would be sad and angry for them leaving me but I wasn't. They probably had a good reason. I mean, who would leave their kid in the middle of the forrest just because?

"Stella!" I heard someone shouting. It was Willow, the woman I called mom. Even though she wasn't my biological mother, she was still like a mother to me.

"What?" I shouted back at her, too lazy to go downstairs. Right before she shouted, the doorbell had rang. There was probably a friend of mine down stairs, having an awkward conversation with Willow as they waited for me.

"Just come down here sweetie," she shouted. I sighed and changed into a pair of jeans and a t-shirt before I slowly made my way downstairs.

At the door I saw my mom talking to a boy. He looked a bit familiar to me, but I couldn't seem to remember his name. It was a quite popular guy from school.

They both noticed me, but stayed talking to each other. Why did she even call me down here if she was going to talk to some douche from my school?

I didn't even bother to listen to their convesartion. Instead I turned around and was just about to go to the kitchen when I was interrupted in my mission.

"Stella," he said. I could still not remember his name but I turned around anyway.

"What?" I asked, sounding a bit cockier than what Willow liked. She glared at me, hinting that I shouldn't be mean to him.

"I was just wondering if we could go out for a walk," he asked trying to sound nice. But no, not in my ears. I came all the way downstairs to have a guy, who I don't even know, to ask me if I wanted to go for a walk. And on top of that, its like 8 am.

My mom gave me a say-yes-now-goddamnit-look, which forced me to say yes. I didn't want her to get any angrier at me, and for some reason it felt like if I said no to this guy she would beat me unconscious. Even though she is one of the kindest people I know.

"Fine," I answered him as I started to put on my worn blue sneakers. Why would this guy even want to do something with me?

We started walking down the silent street. I looked down on my feet, watching our feet walk in rythm toward where ever we were going. My new woken brain still couldn't remember his name, but one thing was for sure, he was not just going to the same school as me.

"So...," he said, wanting to start a conversation. "Uhm..." He could either not come up with anything to say or he forgot what he was going to say.

I looked at the bright blue-eyed blonde boy walking next to me. Still trying to figure out his name.

I wanted to start a conversation with him so he could answer my questions as we talk, without having me asking him. That's what I wished, since I really didn't want to ask for his name.

"Where are we walking?" I asked, blatanly because I really had no idea where he was walking me. He didn't answer.

"Hey, I asked you something," I stopped walking, annoyed that he was the one wanting to strike conversation from the beginning, but when I tried to talk to him he didn't answer. He looked at me with a frown and stopped walking too.

"If I ask you something, you're supposed to answer me," I growled lowly, trying to make it clear that I was annoyed with him.

He gave me a confused face, as if he wondered why I had growled at him. And as I looked into his eyes it hit me.

He was the alphas son.

Chapter 2

"Shit," I whispered quietly hoping that he wouldn't hear me, but by the grin on his face I knew he had heard. This was no good.

How could I forget the name and looks of my Alphas son? The future Alpha of my pack? My best friend's brother? To my defense, I really didn't see him that often.

Despite that, he wasn't answering me! It's his own fault that I almost yelled at him! The fact that he's a prized member of the pack shouldn't give him the privilige to act uncivilized.

"We're not going to any specific place, I just wanted to ask-"

I didn't give him time to finish his sentence and cut him off instead, still as aggrevated as before, though trying to mask it. I didn't want to risk getting punished for behaving inappropriately towards him. "Why couldn't you just have said that in the first place?"

"Because I wanted to keep the it a secret, as well as my intention for this walk," he said, giving me a small smirk. A sign that he had more confidence now than just a minute ago. Back then he didn't know that I had forgotten his name, which was a huge relief to me. Now my ignorance is tugging at my sleeves.

"Can you tell me about that secret now, then?" I spoke back to him in the same fashion. I had calmed down now, but the anger was still bubbling beneath the surface.

"Hm... No," he said with a small shrug. How could anyone possible be this annoying?

Before I could reply to him he spoke again. "Well, it would be a waste of time not to tell you about it now, right?"

Suddenly it felt like he had jumped off his high horse. His cheeks flushed a warmer color as he picked up his words. "My sister is turning fifteen soon and she is having a party... Would you like to go there with me?"

His sister, Madeleine, wasn't his real sister. She was just as me, left by someone in the woods. Madeleine was found three years before me, and she was taken in by the Luna as she had wished for a daughter for a long time.

When Madeleine and I first heard of each other I was six year old and she was eight. The adults always joke around and say that we have been inseparable since then.

Now, when I stant face to face with the boy she calls her brother, I find myself in a cloud of confusion. How could I have forgotten him? And why was he asking me to go to her birthday party with him? If he had been keeping his eyes on me, he would know that I'm a bit of a loner. Maybe this was just a prank?

Although, I knew that Willow, the woman I call mom, wasn't going to be happy at all if I denied his offer. Even if it is a prank, I can't take the risk.

"Okay," I forced myself to say, holding the anger in with all the strength I could muster. Surely the conversation couldn't go on for much longer than that.

Slowly I turned around and started walking back home, feeling the hunger churning deep within.

"Wait, I have some more questions for you," the boy shouted when he realized I was leaving.

"Well, ask them now so I can go home!" I stopped in my tracks to hear what he had to say. Jeez, doesn't he have anything better to do?

A small cough escaped him. His eyes were fixed at the asphalt at his feet, his eyebrows entangled above his eyes. He looked like he was thinking deeply. Surely he must have forgotten about me at this point...

"The adults... They say that your eyes looked like the nightsky. I wanted to know if it was true..."

Pinching the bridge of my nose, I let out a loud sigh. Is he seriously stupid? Did the Luna drop him on his head when he was a little baby? Pointing at my eyes as I stare into his blue ones I groan. "Clearly my eyes are brown!"

I've never seen anyone turn so red in such a short time before. He was quick to hide his head in his hands but I saw his cheeks turn crimson. "I guess rumors are just rumors, then," he mumbled into his hands. "But my parents were really serious when they said so..."

"I've heard that being said, too," I mumble more to myself than to him. Looking up from his hands, his eyes meet mine once again. Ocean blue eyes, displaying confusion.

I could feel my neck heating up a little when I keep speaking, "That's what those eight keep saying, anyway."

"Those eight?" his voice mirroring his eyes - not a single spark of understanding. I can feel my annoyance surfacing again. Oh my God, all these questions. Can't he see that my stomach is eating itself from the inside, and that a big hole soon will appear in my belly and kill me if I don't consume anything soon? Can't he hear the murderous screams and war cries that it keeps letting out?

"Yeah... The ones who saved me that night," I said, hoping he wouldn't ask for more information. But guess what, this isn't really my lucky day.

"Who?" He took a step closer and gave me an enthusiastic glance, begging with his eyes to tell me. Am I hallucinating? Is this really happening? The Alphas son is giving me the puppy eyes.

"My parents and some other people," I said, not really wanting to go into detail. Not only because the details in question weren't really apparent to me, but also because I was getting increasingly annoyed with his presence.

Another growl escaped my stomach, letting me know that breakfast couldn't wait any longer. Slowly I started walking towards my house again.

"Well, I'll see you at the party then, I guess. Say hi to Madeleine from me," I shouted as begun jogging up the street. This time he didn't stop me.

When I spotted the familiar house of mine I started running. My stomach was screaming for food. As I opened the door a familiar scent hit my sensitive nose, my stomach was suddenly howling. Pancakes.

"Hello," I said to Travis, the one I call brother, as I entered the kitchen. He was making pancakes to himself, that selfish little prick. I knew that he would be finished soon when I saw the plate that he was stacking the deliscious buttery pancakes on.

"Don't even think of it," Travis said when he noticed how I looked at the stack.

"Please can I have at least five of them? You already have like twenty!" I begged him, hoping that he was hearing my stomach, begging in unision with me.

"No, they're mine!" He said while putting another one on the stack. "Make your own pancakes if you want them so bad."

"Please Travis! I was shouted at as soon as I woke up and mom forced me to go on a walk with... a guy... And he was really getting on my nerves." I groaned, wanting him to sympathize with me. When I said 'a guy' Travis looked curiously at me. Aha! I managed to peak his interest.

"It was just... the Alpha's son," I murmured very lowly, not wanting him to pay attention to what I was saying. But unfortunately he heard me.

"You did what?!" Travis gave me the biggest frown in response. In his mind he had probably put me in some kind of situation where I was in trouble, so the Alpha had sent his son here to speak with me. If it only were so simple.

"He asked me if I would go on a walk with him, and mom gave me a say-yes-or-I'll-kill-you look so I said yes," I explained, still looking at the pancakes whilst I waved off Travis' shock. He didn't calm down very much, instead he just walked up to me.

"Tell me everything." Travis is one of those overly curious people. Anything could be interesting to him. And when I say anything, I mean it. All the boring things you learn in class are most likely not boring to him.

"Only if I get at least five of those," I said, pointing at the stack of pancakes.

"Fine," he sighed, while laying my pancakes on a plate. Slowly he picked the plate up and placed it in front of me, a small sigh leaving his lips.

"So, tell me everything," Travis is almost like that girly best friend that everyone has. But I don't have anyone like that. Well, you could say that Madeleine's one of those friends too, but she already knows all the details before she has the time to ask for them.

"Okay," I mumbled slowly, "Should I start with the most embarrasing part?"

"Oh, so it was one of those dates," Travis said with a little wink and a smirk plastered onto his stupid face.

"No, it was NOT a date!" Throwing my hands into the air, to look dramatic, I exclaim my displeasure with his words. "He just wanted to go for a walk..."

Travis waved his hand a little to signal that he didn't care.

I look down at the plate and examine the buttery pancakes, feeling my mouth water. The most embarrasing part of the story, huh? I let out a small sigh before I start talking, "I forgot who he was. And I almost started shouting at him! That was when I realized who he was... the Alpha's goddamn son! Of all people!"

"Theo," Travis said amid his own laughter. At least he was enjoying the story.

"What?" I didn't know what he was speaking of.

"His name. You should know that since you and Madeleine are best friends. He's her brother, remember?"

"Yeah, yeah. I know." I groaned, rubbing my eyes. "But back to what happened. He, I mean Theo, noticed when I realized who he was. His whole attitude changed! I've never seen anyone go from chill to acting like they have a stick up their ass before."

Travis laugther came bubbling up quickly. He was clearly amused by my badmouthing of the future Alpha of the pack. I started to giggle as well, even though a joke like that could get me kicked out of the pack if the Alpha were to hear it.

"And you know what's even worse?" I stared my brother deep in the eyes, trying to keep a serious expression. "You know of Maddie's birthday party, right?"

The room felt quiet when his laughter disappeared. Slowly, he nodded. He was probably planning to go there with his mate Dawn. "Yes?"

I tilted my head sligthly, thinking about my brother and his mate. Both him and Dawn are seventeen, whilst I'm thirteen. They always make fun of me for hanging with them instead of people my age. I don't fin it funny at all, in fact, they should be happy that I like them. I don't like many people.

A deep breath.

"He asked me to go to the party with him..."

"And?"

"I said yes," I mumbled, "because mom would have killed me if I said no!" My excuse felt hollow, but it was sort of true. It would be a disgrace to our family if I were to deny the future Alpha. If he were any other person I would have said no in a heartbeat.

My stomach growled loudly. The pancakes looked so tempting, and they disappeared as fast as they had been placed before me.

After I had consumed my breakfast I glanced over at the clock for the first time today. 8:24 am. That means school starts in half an hour.

Oh no. I hate that place.

Chapter 3

"I'm going to school now!" I shouted as I picked up my bag and went outside before anyone could answer me with a "Okay honey, have fun", or a "Are you sure you don't want a ride there?"

I always walk to school. The 20 minute walk refreshes me. It calms my nerves before I have to enter the building where I'll have to endure schoolwork for hours.

The reasons for my burning hate for the place they call "school"? The bullies that don't really bully me, rumors and of course all the rude teachers that decide how many hours I have to be in school. All these precious hours that I had to spend in school. It's a bit sad.

*

The large wooden doors that made up the enterence to the school building were constantly open in the morning. A feeling of dread started growing in the bottom of my stomach. This place didn't make me feel comfortable at all. *

"Hey look, its her," Someone said, I knew he meant me.

"The human," Someone said.

All these rumors about me being an human really wasn't true. No one, besides me, had seen my wolf. And I didn't want anyone to either.

Jokes on them.

But the weird thing was that the first time I shifted was when I just had turned seven.

I remember all that happened that night.

I was trying to sleep but I couldn't.

After my birthday party everyone went to sleep, but I couldn't sleep. I felt weird. Something was wrong.

I went outside, into the forest behind my house. I knew I always got calm when I was here.

Suddenly I felt my bones changing. They were changing positions and some new grow out. I could feel hair growing out from everywhere on my body. I was really scared.

But when I looked down and saw paws, that wasn't what shocked me. It was the color.

Dark, dark blue. Almost black. It was like the color of the night sky above me.

I swiftly got to the lake I knew was a few meters to my right.

I looked at the creature in the reflection in front of me. It was a big wolf. But I could not see the eyes neither their color. All I saw was the sky above me.

I didn't tell anyone what happened that day almost six years ago. Not even Madeleine who was, and is, the closest person to me.

But I still knew that I wasn't supposed to shift into a wolf that early. If I was the first born child I would shift at ten to thirteen and if I wasn't the first born it would've happened when I turn eighteen. But I can, since my 7th birthday, switch into my wolf and speak to her trough my mind.

Her name was Luceat, she had told me that it meant shine in latin. She also asked me if I knew that my name meant star the first time we talked. And oh boy I knew. Everybody had said that to me at least one time before.

"Why are you even in our pack? You aren't even a shifter!" Cindy, the biggest bitch of this school, stopped me. She was fourteen, but she was still a bitch. This was a school whit out any humans in it. It was easy to know, you could not smell any human in miles.

I have never cared about the bullies, they thought I was hurt by them. But nope, not at all. I was just annoyed that they were spending so much time trying to get me hurt.

"Well, Cindy, I am in the pack because they wanted me to be," I responded in hope she would leave me alone.

"And who are 'they'?" She asked, sounded bitchy as normal.

"Well, the alpha and luna," I answered walking to my locker glad she left me alone, this time.

I took out the stuff I needed for my lesson and then walked there. It wasn't gonna start in five minutes so I leaned back at the wall to wait.

Soon the teacher came and opened the door. Quickly I went in to the classroom and sat down at the back as I always did. In a couple of minutes the room was filled whit the people I called classmates.

"Ok," said our teacher, Dennis. "Today we will read page 345 to 357," He said load to make sure everyone heard it.

I opened up my book at page 345. I looked at the pictures on the sides. It were pictures of mythical creatures.

"Why are we gonna read about mythical stuff?" A girl asked. I couldn't remember her name.

Oh gosh! Was I about to forget everybody's names? I can't do that! Oh well, I could always learn them again I guess.

"Just start to read Ms. Winter" Dennis said. He was a good teacher, but he sure didn't look good. He had a big nose whit hairs sticking out of it and eyebrows so far apart that you would wonder how wide his head was. He had a big round belly that almost made him look pregnant. And on top of that; he wore the same clothes all the time.

The rest of the lesson I spent reading about those mythical creatures and greek gods and goddesses. It was quite boring but I guess it is worth knowing, for some stupid reason.

6 hours later

I was now walking home from school. There suddenly was one question circling around my mind. What am I gonna wear tomorrow at Madeleine's party? I might as well ask her.

My phone were soon in my hand, calling Madeleine.

"Hey Stells," She was probably home from school by now. Well why shouldn't she be? Her school day ended an hour ago.

"Hey Maddie, uhm, there was this thing I wanted to ask you about,"

"Well, bring it on," Her voice was filled whit curiosity.

"Uhm, so what do you want me to wear for your party tomorrow?" I asked.

"Are you home right now?" Why would she ask that..?

"In like a minute or so... Wh-"

"Cause Im coming over" Her voice sounded a bit evil in some way. I couldn't argue whit her because she had already dropped the call.

I guess she is going to pick an outfit for me.

Chapter 4

The second I stepped into the house I got dragged up into my room. That got me wondering how long Madeleine had been in here for.

"Well, I am forced to wear a dress by my mom," She said sitting down on my bed. I could tell that she was very disappointed. Both of us hated wearing dresses.

"So I will choose clothes for you instead," She said whit an evil smirk on her face.

"Im not so sure about that," I said making her look even more disappointed.

"You'll have to have my agreement on what to wear," That made the evil smirk grow back on her face.

Oh god.

Okay so, first of all, you need to look pretty ass hell but whit out wearing a dress," She said as she were looking trough my wardrobe. Even though we both hated wearing dresses we loved how pretty they were.

"Maybe this shirt. No wait, this one! Nah...,"

After two hours she was satisfied whit a pair of black ripped jeans and a grey t-shirt whit a white text saying "Hands off" on it.

After two freaking hours?!? She was a really crazy person when it comes to clothes. But after all, she was going to wear a dress on her party.

"This. Is. Perfect." She said when she saw me wearing it after she forced me to put it on. I knew this would look super good on her. On me? I don't know.

'I think your pretty' It was my wolf, Luceat. She didn't really speak that much.

"Well then you should be even more happy when Im saying I'll wear it to your party," And she was. I could see the happiness growing inside of her. And on top of that she had a gigantic smile taped onto her face.

"Yay! I wish I could be here before the party, making sure you will look pretty as heck, but unfortunately mom forces me to stay home," She sounded a bit sad when she said that. And the smile and happiness was slowly leaving her body.

"Yeah... But we'll se each other at the party, right?" I said in hope that she would get happy, and she did.

"Ya," she said and nodded whit a little smile on her lips.

"So how do you feel about the 'your meeting you mate tomorrow' thing?" In the twelve years she have lived here she got to know that she was the child of an alpha, but they could never find the parents nor the pack. And that means she is meeting her mate when shes fifteen. Which means that she is meeting him (or her) tomorrow.

"I am so so so so exited. You wouldn't understand!" Se sounded super happy.

"But you are so ugly though," I began. Jokingly of course. She was stunning. Whit that long brown hair of hers and those perfectly straight teeth in her mouth.

"Your mate will probably reject you at first sight," I finished. And soon my body was on the floor whit an angry Madeleine over me. All I did was laughing.

"Take that back!" She said. I knew that she was very angry for what I said but she knew that I was joking.

"No," I said while shaking my head. I shouldn't had said that. As soon as I said it Madeleine was starting to tickle me.

"Okay! Okay, your mate is not going to reject you," I laughed as she stopped tickling me.

"Thats more like it," she laughed. But to be honest, I was kinda scared that she would meet her mate tomorrow. What if she left the pack to be whit him? What if she stopped being whit me because of him? What if he rejects her and she becomes a crying ball of sadness?

"Hey, why you looking all sad all of a sudden?" She asked, worryingly.

"It was just the thought of you leaving the pack or me for your mate..." As I said that she looked at me whit a smile.

"I would never leave you," She embraced me and I hugged her back.

"Maybe the Moon Goddess doesn't have a mate for you," I laughed. She shook her head, still whit that same smile of hers.

As soon as we went to stand up her phone rang. She excused herself to go answer the call as I sat down on my bed.

In what I believed was a minute she got back from the call.

"Mom called, I need to go home," I nodded at her and she hugged me once again.

"Bye," We both said at almost the same time.

But then I remembered a thing, I didn't have a birthday present for her birthday tomorrow.

"Maddie, what do you want for your birthday?" I asked.

She chuckled but then she answered. "You don't have to give me anything," She said before she left.

Well, she is not gonna be happy if I come to the party whiteout a present.

2 hours later

After I rushed to the mall to find something for Madeleine I went in almost every store there was.

Then I figured I could just give her a mug. Because who doesn't want a mug? Well, yeah, maybe your not like "Wow! Thank you, I love you for buying a mug for me!" when you get a mug, but everybody knows that when you need a mug - there is no clean mug there.

I went into a second hand store and bought a plane white mug whit a text on it, after I'd read the text I instantly bought it.

"I <3 mugs. (Not really, but I wanted something whit 'I <3' on this mug but I couldn't figure out what to write)"

It was probably someone who had designed it in a web shop of some sort. But the text was slightly funny, and I think Maddie will love it.

As I came home I heard Willows voice scream at me."Stella! Where have you been? I was so worried!" Overprotective much?

"I was at the mall getting a birthday present for Maddie," I said and showed them the bag I had the mug in.

"Well, you have to call next time," Willow said angrily.

"Sorry," Then I went upstair a d into my room. I didn't want to eat dinner today.

I showered and then changed into my pj's.

What an eventful day...

Chapter 5

I looked up. The woman who was running with me looked really focused. On what she was focused on? I don't really know.

Suddenly she just stopped. I looked around to see where we were.

In front of me there was a big three story house. It was very familiar, but I felt like it was the first time seeing it.

The woman started walking again. We got inside of the house. It was very warm inside, I liked it.

A man looked down on me. He wasn't there in the forest. Who was he?

"We found it in the forest, alpha," The woman started and then smiled at me."It was going to die if we didn't take it home whit us." She looked up at the man again.

"Well, didn't your son want a sibling?" He asked.

"Do you mean tha-"

"Yes, you'll have to take care of it." The man said.

I felt sleepy, so I closed my eyes.

"Stella! School starts in half an hour!" Travis screamed, waking me up.

Quickly I got up and ran to my wardrobe. After a minute or so I had picked a pair of blue jeans and a black t-shirt. Then I put everything on, brushed my hair and teeth and ran downstairs.

I took a pear from the fruit bowl and took a bite as I put on my shoes.

"Bye!" I said. But I had forgotten my bag, so I ran in again.

"Are you sure you don't want a ride there? You know I have my motorcycle in the garage." Travis said giggling at me running around looking for my bag.

"Nah, Im fine." I answered. Where could my bag be? I left it here yesterday!

"But then I'll don't give you your bag." I stopped and slowly turned around. There Travis stood holding my bag and a helmet.

"Fine," I said and took both the bag and the helmet. Then we walked out to the garage. I stood there watching Travis pull the motorcycle out.

"Jump on and hold onto me if you don't wanna fall off." Travis said.

I put on my helmet and then jumped on. Travis started driving quite slow, I didn't know why though. Both me and Travis loved speed.But when he realized how slow we were driving he sped up.

When we were in the school parking I jumped off. I took off the helmet and said goodbye to Travis.

When I was inside of the school Cindy came up to me. She thought that she were a super cool bully. But that wasn't the case. She was more like someone who tried to be mean but wasn't any good at it.

"Hey! You!" She said in her annoying high pitch voice.

"What?" I asked her.

"You look super ugly today!" Was she really trying to get me sad? Because it doesn't work that way.

"Well I know. You too." I said.

"What?!? Me, ugly?!? Never! I am the definition of perfect!" She screamed. More like the definition of why people are deaf.

"Sure, sure." I said walking to my locker. She was a crazy human being.

"Yes she is." Her friend Olivia said. What? Is she brainwashed or something? Olivia sometimes talked to me when Cindy wasn't there. We both hated Cindy. Just the way she behaved and how stupid she is is one thing to hate her for.

I rolled my eyes as I opened my locker. Olivia rarely said something when Cindy tried to 'bully' me. She behaved quite strange today. And she looked quite strange too. Olivia always had jeans and t-shirts, like me. But today she had a crop-top and a short skirt. Did Cindy force her to wear that?

"Cindy is super good looking!" Okay, Olivia is brainwashed.

I took out the stuff I needed for my lesson and walked past them. Taking a look at Olivia I saw that she was very uncomfortable with what she was wearing. Maybe she wasn't that brainwashed.

"Where are you going ugly?!?" The voice was still super high pitched. Can't Cindy speak like a normal person? This is hurting my ears.

"To my lesson. Bye uglier." I said. New nicknames huh?

As I left I heard Cindy talking angrily about me to Olivia and her other friend Wilma.

"Today we are going to do a spelling test," The teacher said with his weird accent. I sometimes wonder where he comes from. He told us once, but I don't have the best memory so of course I had forgotten.

"I will say the word in a sentence and then say which word you will write." He said as he gave us a paper each. Maybe he was russian? Bulgarian? Chinese? Danish? Who knows?

"My car is red, write car" Does he think we're stupid? Everybody can spell car! Ever three year olds!

The lesson was super boring. It was the teacher saying words we had to write down. Mostly super easy words like "cat" and "giraffe".

At lunch I sat down by myself, Madeleine went to the same school as me but she had lunch in an hour or so. So I sat down by myself and looked down at the food. Our school actually had quite good food. Today we got some kind of soup whit mushrooms in. Unfortunately I hate mushroom.

A plate were put down in front of me. I looked up and saw an unfamiliar face smiling at me.

"Hi?" I said, but it sounded more like a question.

"Hi Im new here. Amelia." She introduced herself. I put a smile on my lips, to be nice of course.

"Stella," I said and she sat down. She was kind of cute whit her orange hair that looked a bit more brown than orange, and her freckles all over her face. Her hair was curly.

"So, did you move here or did you just change school?" I asked to start a conversation whit her.

"I moved here last week." She said looking down in her food whit a disgusted expression on her face.

"Its ok, I don't like mushroom soup either." I said laughing. And she started laughing too.She smelled like a wolf, and so she was.

"We just joined this pack I can't remember what its called..." She said.

"Paper moon?" I asked. That was my pack. The name was a bit weird, I mean paper moon? The moon isn't made of paper.

"Yeah!" She said happily.

"Well then you're in my pack," I said and she looked smiling at me again.

"Yay! I got so worried that I wouldn't get any friends in the pack," She said and looked super happy.

"Well tomorrow, or later today in school, we can go and be whit my best friend a bit. It would be awesome if you could be friends too!" I said imagining us being super duper good friends together.

Amelia nodded."We could go outside before lunch is over?" I asked her and she nodded.

We went outside and sat underneath a big oak."So are you able to shift or are you not?" She asked me.

"I can shift, but the rumors say that Im human." I said and chuckled.

"Hm... Okey. I can shift too. My wolf is grey whit green-ish eyes. How does yours look?" She asked. I smiled. "Nobody but me knows, but I guess you can know too. But keep it a secret, alright?" I said.

"I promise." She smiled.

"Its super dark blue, like the nightsky." I said looking at my hands.

"Is that even possible?" She asked.

"I guess so, because my wolf certainly is blue..." I said.

"What about the eyes?" She asked. Yeah, what about them? I couldn't see them.

"I don't know..." I said looking up on a branch.

"You don't know?" She asked.

"I just saw the sky, super weird I know." I said.

"Hm..." She murmured. She was probably as confused as I.

Then we heard a bell ring, the lunch was over. The rest of the lessons were fast and now I stood at my locker, taking out my bag.

"Im gonna be at your house at six." I heard a voice whisper in me left ear. Theo.

Chapter 6

When I came home I rushed up to my room and took a look at my clock. 3:45 pm.

I put on the clothes Madeleine had picked out for me and then took the bag whit the mug in.

"Who lives in a pineapple under the sea?

Spongebob squarepants!"

Yes, I watched spongebob. But when your thirteen you are considered as a kid, so you can in fact watch kid programs.

I watched spongebob until 5:34 when Travis came home.

"Where have you been?" I asked him.

"At school." He said, trying to avoid the conversation. It was obvious that he had been whit Dawn, probably at her house.

"And you came home now? No, you must have been somewhere else... Oh! You were at Dawn's house!" I said as I ran away into the kitchen where he was.

"Maybe..." He said.

"Maybe? Well ok then." I said and took an apple.

"Okey, I was at her house. But she needed to fix herself for Mad's party." He looked a bit sad. Obviously because he wanted to be whit her right now.

"And I needed to get her present so I went home,"

"What did you get her?" I asked curiously. I hope he bought her clothes, something good looking that I could steal. Well, even though it would be hers I always take her stuff.

"I wont tell you. You will just tell Madeleine about it and ruin it," He said.

Ding Dong the doorbell shouted.

I went to the door and opened it. There stood Theo whit a smile on his face. He wore jeans and a tee.

"Hi," He said.

"Hey," I said and took a step out from the house whit the bag in my hand. "Bye!" I screamed to Travis an closed the door. Mom and dad were probably at the party already.

"Let's go then," The said and we started walking.

Unfortunately it was a five minute walk to the party, way to long. I didn't really like Theo, we were barely friends. I was quite shocked when he wanted me to go whit him to the party.

"So... What did you buy for her?" Theo asked. I don't know if I should tell him or not.

"If you are that type of person who tells the one getting the present what I bought, then I bought a present," I said as I looked down at the ground. Just two more minutes until were there.

"But what if Im not that kind of person?" It sounded like a question, but I was not sure if it was one.

"Then I wouldn't tell you either," I said and started walking a bit faster.

"There the party is," He said and I looked at the house. It had a banner on it saying "Happy 15th Birthday Madeleine!"

We walked into the house. There were not many people in here, but the party was about to start.

"Hi!" We heard a voice say and soon Madeleine stood in front of us.

'You and Theo, huh' She mind-linked me. She was the only one I mind-linked.

'Well, if I would've said no mom would've killed me!' I said back. And she started laughing.

"Why are you laughing?" Theo asked Madeleine making her laugh even more.

"Heres your present," I said as I wave her the bag. She took the bag and opened it.

"A mug?" She asked.

"Yeah, thats all you deserve," I said laughing. But after she'd read what the mug said she laughed too. Theo was confused so he walked over to his parents to talk to them instead.

"Thank you," Madeleine said and hugged me."I better go and welcome the other guests," She said and walked away, leaving me alone.

I walked over to Willow who was putting up decorations.

"Hey sweetie," She said and patted my head.

"Hi, what are you doing?" I asked looking up to see her face. She was standing on a little ladder, to reach further up, putting up the decorations in the box at the table on her left. I didn't really know why I asked that, I mean I already knew what she was doing...

"Putting up decorations," She said as she taped a purple sparkling thing onto the wall. Even though the party already had started they were still putting up decorations. Didn't they do this yesterday? This seems a bit unplanned.

"Look, Madeleine's mate!" My moms finger pointed behind me. I turned around to see a boy, the same age as Madeleine, from our pack. Wow. He had brown hair, as her, whit a pair of green eyes. Just looking at him made me hope that when I found my mate he would be just as good looking. And nice of course. Its very important that he will be nice.

"Why don't you go speak whit him," My mom said, still putting up the decorations. Yeah, I will need to see if he is nice. If not I don't think he would suit Maddie.

"Hi," I said as I was in front of him. At first he was a bit confused, but the he saw that it was me who had spoken. Didn't he notice me standing in front of me? Oh well.

"Hi," He said and smiled shyly. So he was one of the shy ones, huh?

"So you're Madeleine's mate?" I asked whit an innocent smile. He obviously didn't know that I was her bffff (best fucking friend for fucking ever). He nodded. Good, he knew that.

"So, you like her?" I asked making him nod again. Was he mute? No he couldn't be, he said hi to me. He was just one of those shy ones. Or he was just new around, I haven't seen him before.

"Good, cause you know, if you hurt her you'll be dead," I said and stretched out my hand for him to shake.

"Madeleine's best friend, Stella," I said whit that same innocent smile. He looked at me as if I was an alien and then he shook my hand.

"Yosef," He said. After he let go of my hand two arms were rapped around his waist. He looked calm.

"I see you two are coming along?" Maddie said. I nodded and smiled. He looked at me and nodded slowly. But then something very unexpected happened. I felt something splash onto my back. Probably some kind of drink. I growled and turned around. Shocked was not what I was, seeing Theo whit a cup in his hand. He was shocked.

"Argh!" I began. Why did he throw a cup of... Whatever that liquid was... On my back?!?"I feel sorry for the girl that will get to know shes your mate!" I screamed and ran out of the building. And the words were true, every single one of them. That girl, whoever she will be, Im sorry for.

Chapter 7

Almost two years ago I remember storming out of a party, running straight home packing my bags. I also remember taking my helmet and stealing my brothers motorbike and driving away from my pack, and the city. After seeing him riding on it and myself trying going on it, I knew how to drive it.

I remember that I stopped right outside a pack house. Then I fell down on the grown, how far was I from home? I didn't know.

Two years ago I remember waking up in a hospital. Their pack doctor said to me that I was so exhausted I fell down on the ground and fell asleep.

"Hey, shes awake," I heard someone saying as I slowly opened my eyelids. They felt super heavy for some reason. But when I finally opened my eyes I took a look at my surroundings. I was in a hospital looking room, white walls and ceiling.

"Where am I?" I asked as I saw a woman and a man holding hands a few meters to my left. The man radiated power, he must be an alpha and the woman must be his luna.

"At the blood moon packs hospital," The man said calmly. I looked around once again and saw the doctor. My head was slightly aching, probably because the pillow my head was laying on was more like a piece of fabric.

"Now when you're awake we need to know what pack you came from, so we can get you back home," The luna said walking to the chair on the left side of the bed. As she sat dow she looked at me, waiting for me to confess where I was from.

"No. I am not going back there. Never," I said shaking my head.

I can't remember anything else from that day.

Now, almost two years later, I was still staying at that pack. But all that time I've felt guilt. I've felt guilt because I left. I mean, why did I even leave? Anger issues? No, just anger. But I have, ever since that day, been wanting to go back. So badly.

I just wanted a hug from mom again, a pat on the shoulder by dad. I even miss those glares from Travis. And the worst thing was; I even missed Cindy.

But I couldn't go back. Everyone would say things like "Why did she even come back? We don't want her here anymore" or "Your family got so sad they killed themselfs". Okey, maybe not that last one.

I knew I had to go back. Even if I wanted it or not. So I wrote a note to everyone that I cared about over here. As I stared out and up on the night sky I wondered what to write.

"Please don't be sad for me leaving. You already knew I would do it some time... After two years, I've kinda gotten insane... I know it sounds crazy, but Im dying to find what my family and best friend have done under these past two years. I love y'all, I promise to come visit once in a while!

xoxo Stella"

I left the note on my desk in my little room. I had already packed my bags a few days ago. I took them and ran out of the house, to my motorcycle.

I put on the helmet and made sure that the bags wouldn't fall off. Then I started driving.

Two hours later I was at my old house, super nervous. I knew that they probably were asleep rightnow, midnight and all. But still, this is quite important.

I knocked on the door. No one answered. I rang the doorbell.

"Who the hell is at our door now?" I heard an angry voice say from inside. It sounded just like Willows.The door slowly opened.

"Stella?" She froze. What was I going to say? "Hey, I know I left you like a little more than one and a half years ago, but Im back now. Ayye!!!" No.

"Hi," I said shyly. Looking down at my feet.

"Willow, who are you talking to?" I heard footsteps, and now two people stood frozen in front of me.

'Awkwaaaaaard' I heard Luceat say. Well, I have to admit that she is right.

"Oh my god we thought you were dead!" Willow hugged me, hard, as if she never wanted to let go of me, maybe because she thought I would run away again.

"Well, Im not," I said with an awkward laughter and hugged her back. Breathing in that strawberry sent of hers. Oh god, I've missed that.

"Travis!" Connor (the man I called dad) shouted. I heard a big groan before the stair started creaking. Then I heard some steps in the hall before another person froze.

"Stella?" He asked, his eyebrows seemed like they touched eachother. I just smiled at him. And he knew that it was me.

"Where have you been? I was so freaking worried!" He said and ran forward to me. And then he crashed into me in a hug. I chuckled and hugged him back. How was I going to explain it all?

I shook my head whit a big smile on my lips. I've missed them so much. Right now I felt so much happiness.

"Well Im back now..." I said still smiling. "And I thought you might wanted your motorcycle back," Pointing towards the motorcycle. Travis eyebrows flew up, it almost looked like they were going to be ripped out of his head and fly up to space.

"You're probably super tired," Willow said and made some room for me to come in. I went back to the motorbike and got my bags and then walked in. Everything was almost exactly like the day I left. My steps directed me up the stairs and into my room. It was almost the same as before, besides that it was cleaned. I remember leaving it really messy. But I didn't know that I was leaving though. I just left because I was so angry. Maybe I overreacted a bit...

I put down my bags at the floor. I was too tired to do anything more than brush my teeth. And that was the only thing I did before I laid down in my bed and fell asleep. I didn't even change into my pj's.

Goodnight, I thought to myself before I was sleeping.

Chapter 8

When I woke up I went straight into the bathroom. Took off my clothes, jumped in the shower, took a quick shower and wrapped myself in a towel. Then I looked at myself in the mirror.

My light blue eyes was staring back at me. The hair which once was brown wasn't. A year ago I dyed it dark, dark, blue. Almost like the color of my wolfs fur. It was still straight as before, but it was longer. Almost down to my belly button. Under this time being away I had turned fifteen. I was much longer, maybe fifteen centimeters. My face didn't look like a little kids, it looked more like a womans. My hands and feet got bigger too, not much though.

When I was back in my room I changed into a grey t-shirt and a pair of dark blue jeans.

When I was done whit fixing myself I went downstairs to get something to eat. I found an apple and Travis in the kitchen. Of course he noticed me.

"You've changed your hair," He said as he noticed my new hair color. I nodded and took a bite of the apple I was holding.

"You look tired," I pointed out. He looked really tierd, like he hadn't slept anything last night.

"Yeah, I mean, someone rang the doorbell in the middle of the night," He said looking at me. I glared at him and then I went to put on my shoes.

"Where are you going?" Willow asked as she was coming out from her room. Her hair was a mess and she looked tired too.

"Out, to get some fresh air," I said as I began putting on my left shoe.

"Then you can go and buy some milk and fruits?" She asked, I knew that she would force me to either way.

"Sure," I said and went into the kitchen again. Willow was holding some dollar bills. I took them before leaving the house.

Twenty minutes later I was in town hoping no one would recognize me. As if the world had heard my wish, nobody who I recognized recognized me. Probably because my new hair color and how much I had grown.

I walked inside of the little shop that I knew sold fruits and milk, but also other things like weapons, chairs, tables and docrations.

When I grabbed a package of milk I could smell something that smelled like mint. I love mint...

I followed the smell and stopped some meters away. There were some teenage boys standing looking at the fruits, probably the same age as me. I stopped by the vegetables and looked away. One of the guys smelled like mint, and something else. Almost like... Pizza. Another thing that I love. This is weird...

"Hey there," The boy who smelled like mint and pizza said. It felt like I had heard that voice before, but at the same time it felt like it was the first.

I slowly turned my head and saw a guy that looked super familiar. Where did I know him from?

"Uhm, hi," I said, still trying to figure out who he was. He was defiantly a werewolf, so was the other guys that stood some meters behind him.

"Your new here?" He asked. What should I answer? "No I left almost two years ago and came back last night, you look familiar... Whats your name?" Nah, that just sounds weird.

"Hm," I said instead. He looked at me whit confusion in his eyes. They were really, really pretty.

"Theo," He said and smiled.

Oh god. That Theo. The guy who I never wanted to see again.

"Shit," I said and shoved my hand up my hair. Thats why he smelled so good. I was his mate. Fuck.

"What?" He asked. This was a nightmare. Why was he even exciting? Can't that pretty boy just disappear and never come back again? Like I did.

'But he's our mate...' Luceat reminded me. I know that.Why me? The Moon Goddess must be sick or something...

"Im sorry for the girl that will get to know shes your mate!"

My words echoed in my head. I was that poor girl.

"Stella," I said coldly. He looked really shocked. His friends too.

I leaned forward to whisper in his ear. "I reject you," I whispered and he froze. Then I walked away to the apples.

"What did she say?" One of Theo's friends asked him.

"Dude, you ok?" The other one asked. In the corner of my eye I saw Theo still standing frozen, but he had turned around and was now staring at me.

I picked up four apples and laid them in a plastic bag before going to the checkout and paying for them and the milk.

So Theo has turned fifteen?

20 minutes later

"Im home!" I said when I came home. After my shoes were off I went straight to the kitchen where Willow stood and gave her the bag.

"We were wondering if you maybe wanted to go to Theo's 15th birthday party?" Willow asked shyly. I didn't answer at first, but then I realized that Maddie probably would be there.

"Okay..." I said and Willow smiled. It will be super awkward meeting Theo after what happened in the store, but I really wanted to meet Maddie.

"Were going there in an hour," Willow said. An hour? I looked up at the clock on the wall. 4.20 pm.

I walked up the stairs and inside my room. I didn't bother to change clothes so instead I put some mascara on.

My face was quite pale, but I didn't have acne or any weird spots to cover up. Before I walked down again I put on sine deodorant.

I walked into the living room to see everyone sitting in the sofa waiting for me.

"Let's go then," Travis said and they all stood up and started walking to the hall. I put my sneakers on and walked out waiting fir the others.

We started walking and it only took us seven minutes to come to the house. When we stepped in I saw Madeleine and her mate sitting down at a table.

"Go talk to her," Willow said and gave my back a push away against her.

"Stella?!?" Madeleine was fast up on her feet whit her hans on my shoulders. Why does everyone have to get so shocked seeing me?

"Hi," I said smiling shyly at her.

"Oh my god! Where have you been? Weren't you like dead or something?" She asked and hugged me.

"No, I was just at another pack," I said and she got a bit calmer.

"We thought you were dead!" She said and I could see tears forming in her eyes.

"Who?" I asked. Who would think I was dead?

"Everybody thought so!" I could see the tears running down her cheeks. She must've been so sad.

"Madeleine, why are you crying?" It was Rachel, the luna, who talked. Madeleine just pointed at me making Rachel angry.

"Why did you make her cry?" Rachel asked me. So she doesn't recognize me, huh?

"Mom," Madeleine said looking up at Rachel. They went quiet for a bit, probably mind linking.

"Stella?!?" Rachel suddenly screamed, making everyone look at me.

"Yeah...?" I answered and she hugged me.

"You should go and congratulate Theo, he would be happy seeing you here," Rachel said. And why would I want to do that? But she probably doesn't know about what happened in the store.

"N-" She didn't let me finish, instead she just dragged me to Theo.

'This will be fun to watch' Luceat said. I cut her off. No, it will absolutely not be fun.

"Theo, look who's here!" Rachel said happily. Theo froze when he saw me, and I glared at him. Rachel looked confused.

I walked back to my parents.

'Please go back! I want to talk to our mate!' Luceat complained.

'No, I don't want to talk with him' I answered then I cut her off.

Chapter 9

"Thank you for coming here today to our son Theo's 15th birthday party," Jaxon, the alpha of our pack, said as he held his arms around Rachel.

"So, tell us now, have you found your mate?" Jaxon asked him. Theo looked super uncomfortable as he stood there whit all the people in the room staring at him.

He nodded slowly as he looked down at his feet. I couldn't help to feel a little bad for him.

"Where is she?" Jaxon asked. Theo bit his lip and then took a deep breath. "Dad... She rejected me..." Theo said. I heard gasps all around the room.

"Who would reject a soon to be alpha?" I heard someone murmur. Me. I would. Or, I did.

"What?" Jaxon said angrily. I smiled a bit. "She did what?" Jaxon asked again when his son wouldn't answer.

"She rejected me," Theo said a bit more confident. He now looked up at his dad.

"Who is this girl?" Jaxon asked. He was super angry. Please, please don't say my name Theo! My life would be ruined.

But to my luck Theo just shook his head. Medeleine, who stood next to me, seemed a bit angry too.

'Why are you angry?' I mind linked her and she looked at me.

'Because the girl who was meant to be our future luna and my brothers mate rejected him!' She answered as if it was obvious. I just mentally rolled my eyes at it. Well yeah, its kind of stupid ti reject a soon-to-be alpha but I really don't like Theo.

Jaxon looked like he could go up on the roof and just simply stomp the building down at any moment. Thankfully Rachel was there to calm him. I couldn't hear what they were saying even though I tried listening.

"We need to find this girl and talk to her," Jaxon raised his voice, probably getting angrier. Oh god, this is it. Theo is going to point me out and Jaxon is going to rip my face of and make it a decoration to have in his living room.

"Is she from the pack?" Jaxon asked Theo, who still stood awkwardly in a uncomfortable position. My wolf wanted to go and wrap our arms around him, but that would be super weird. Plus, they would find out that I am that girl Jaxon wants to kill. Or maybe Im overreacting a bit.

Theo nodded slowly and bit his lip. I felt a bit sad for him, I had ruined his birthday party for gods sake!

"Is she in this room?" Jaxon asked him. There was not many girls in here, perhaps fifteen. And at least eight of them had mates.

"Dad," Theo said and looked at his father. "Calm down," He said. But Jaxon won't calm down in quite some time. I just want to leave this room and get some fresh air right now. But I can't, it will seam too suspicious.

Jaxon punched a hole in a wall and left. Leaving Theo all by himself, with everybody staring at him. "Awkward," I heard Martin, Theo's best friend say. Everybody started to laugh, leaving the tense feeling behind us.

"Open your presents dude!" His other friend said. After almost two years being away from here I seem to have forgotten his name.

"Yeah," Theo said as he walked to the table where all his presents laid. He picked up a box rapped in some kind of purple paper and started to rip it opened. Inside of the box was a pair of black vans. He opened the rest of the presents and thanked people for them. Travis gave him a pillow whit his face on it as a "prank".

The rest of the presents I didn't really care about. Instead I went out to get that fresh air I so desperately wanted a minute ago. I breathed in the oxygen as I was standing against the house wall.

"What are you doing outside? The party is in there," A familiar voice said.

"Sorry for ruining your party," I said and he let out a laugh. This party wasn't really going to be the party you reminded as "It was super fun, with no flaws at all!" it was going to be reminded as "The awkward party whit a dad who rage quitted".

"Its okey..." He stood just about a meter to my left. We were both looking out against the road. "I ruined Madeleine's 15th birthday part," He stated.

"In which way did you ruin hers?" I looked up at his eyes but honestly I wish I wouldn't have. Instead I looked back at the road in front if the house.

"After throwing that mug of soda on you, not on purpose though, and you stormed out Maddie got so mad at me. She wouldn't even talk to me for almost a week." He said as it was the worst thing that could ever happen to him.

"Theo!" One of his friends shouted from the house door, wanting him to come in. It is his party after all.

"I better be going. Bye," He said and leaned towards me. Perhaps to kiss me. Didn't he know what it meant to be rejected? He must know, but maybe the thought of me being able to give him a change even though I rejected him might have given him some hope. But no, I am not giving him a change. Instead I backed away a few steps. "Bye," I said as I slowly started walking home. No way I was going to stay here at this boring party, which I clearly ruined.

... Whit out anyone knowing it was me. That sounds really weird when I say it.

As I walked beside the road kicking a stone I heard a car. It drove some meters in front of me before stopping. Is this when I get kidnapped by some creepy dude and he almost kills me and then some hot guy comes in saving me like it is some kind of book? No, that doesn't happen in real life... I think.

I stopped walking in my thoughts and got back to reality. The red Volvo, which looked really old, was standing still. I couldn't see the driver through the dark windows.

"Stella?" I heard someone saying after the back door of the car opened. Jeez, people are really wearing my name out. Now I get why people say "Yes, thats my name. Don't wear it out" because thats whats happening with mine.

"Stella? Is that you?" The girl who stood in front of me wasn't one I recognized. She was really pretty though.

"It depends on how many Stella's you know," I answered and took a glance at her. She had a lot of freckles and her hair was brown-ish. It was kind of orange too. For some reason I didn't recognize her, but apparently she recognized me.

"I only know one. But one day she disappeared," The girl said. So she knew me? Why couldn't I remember her then? "You look just like her, except the hair. She had dark brown hair and not blue," She stated pointing at my hair whit her finger.

"Maybe she dyed it?" I said making her stare at me. It was really cold outside and it started to get dark. Everything I want right now is to cuddle up in my bed and sleep for the whole night and day. Even though its school tomorrow, and I will probably get forced to go there.

"Oh my god. Its really you!" She was really happy by the looks of it. Too bad I can't remember her.

"Soooo... I've forgotten loads of names and faces..." I began. This girl looked to be the same age as me, I hope she is going to the same school as I went to before. So I will have at least one friend.

"Oh, Im sorry. I was new at school when you disappeared. But we sat together at lunch and we talked about our wolves... Amelia," We looked at each other for a bit. So I've told her about my wolf? Then she must be the only one who knows about how it looks.

"Amelia! Mom is waiting for us to come pick her up!" A guy shouts from the car. He is probably the one driving.

"Coming!" She shouted back at him. "Bye, I'll see you in school?"

"Yeah," I answer as she goes back to the car. That was weird.

Chapter 10

I stepped inside of the house I once called mine. I don't know what to think of it now. Am I even going to stay here for so long? At least I will go back multiple times a month, to the blood moon pack. They wouldn't be happy if I just left and never visited again to go back to the place where I grew up. Right now they are probably really sad. Even though I never joined their pack I was one of the best fighters there.

"Where have you been?" Willow asked me. I looked at the clock on the kitchen wall after I had taken off my shoes. 22:18 pm.

"The past day people have been recognizing me you know. So a car stopped and a girl came out and asked me lots of stuff," I answered her. Right now my body just wanted sleep, sleep and even more sleep.

"Goodnight," She placed a kiss on my forehead as she embraced me. I hugged her back and murmured a "goodnight" back to her and walked up to my room.

The toothbrush I used to use before I left was still in the bathroom. Thats kind of gross. Who would keep an old toothbrush thats not going to be used for god knows how long? This family!

I brushed my teeth and changed into my pajamas then I went to bed. As I closed my eyes I could feel how exhausted I was. Then I fell asleep.

"Hey baby girl" A woman was holding me in her arms. She poked my nose gently and smiled at me.

"Mom! Look at her eyes!" A little boy to the woman's left said. He was bending over to look at me. The boy couldn't be over two and a half years old.

"They are pretty, aren't they?" She asked whit her soft voice. The boy looked at the woman and nodded. He stared at me, especially my eyes.

"It looks like she has stars in her eyes, mom!" The boy said loudly. The woman hushed at him and looked down at me.

"Yes, it does look like they have stars in them," She said calmly and smiled at me.

I sat up. That dream, I haven't had it for years. Why was it coming back?

"School is in half an hour," Travis said as he walked past my door. Half an hour?

I went straight into the shower and washed my body quickly. Wrapped in a towel I rushed back into my room and chose clothes. I went for some ripped black jeans and a black t-shirt. I left my hair as it was after brushing it and brushing my teeth I went downstairs.

"Good morning," Travis said as he was eating some cereal. I rolled my eyes and went to look in the fridge, only to find out it was empty. Or just filled with things you couldn't eat for breakfast.

"What are you even eating cereal with?" I asked Travis. There was no yoghurt or milk home at the moment. He smiled at me. What did that mean?

"Water," He said chuckling. He knew how much I hated people who eat cereal with water.

"Euwww!" I said and went to look in the fruit bowl. My hand grabbed a banana and pealed it.

"You know, mom and dad got me a new motorcycle when you left with mine," Travis looked up from the discussing cereal and water mix. "So you can have the old one," He finished.

"Yes!" I said and threw the banana peal into the trashcan as I walked to the hall. I put on my shoes and a jacked.

"Bye!" I shouted, to let everyone in the house know that I was about to leave. The motorbike helmet went on my head and I turned on the motorbike.

"Let's go to school then," I murmured as I sat down on the bike and started driving to the building.

The familiar surroundings made me wanna puke. This wasn't really bringing up those good memories. Just the ones in which I had terrible headaches when I went home from school.

The school still looked the same. It was still made out of bricks, it still had a roof. Why wouldn't it though? It had the same parking as before.

Lots of people looked at me as I drove into the parking and parked my bike. They probably thought "A new girl? Cool!" or something similar. But jokes on them: Im not new here.

I locked the motorbike onto some kind of railing and then took off my helmet. It wasn't really comfortable to be stared at, so I went into the school building. As I walked to the principals office I looked down at the floor. Mainly because I didn't want anyone to see my face and stop me as I walked.

I knocked on a door whit a sign which said Principles office. Immediately I heard someone shout "Come in!". It was a woman.

"Stella?" She asked, sounding really confused. This was probably going to be my week: people asking if I was who I was and why I was here.

"Yes. I am back. I would like to get my schedule and a new locker, if you have given mine away," I said and she nodded.

"Of course," She was still confused. I took a look at her. She was still a middle age woman with boring clothes.

A few minutes later she handed me some papers. "Heres your new locker and its code, as well as your schedule,"

I started walking to the locker. It was a few spaces from my old one. When I found it I opened it. It was empty. I left my jacket and my backpack in there and started walking to the classroom. Everybody was probably already in there, which means that I probably will be stared at.

Slowly I opened the door and everyone looked at me. "Hi, are you new here?" The teacher asked me. I stood against the wall.

"Not really, but I haven't been here for almost two years or so," I said. Everybody started whispering. It doesn't look like they recognize me. I recognized most of them.

"Whats you name?" A guy asked. He was very long and muscular. It looked like he was popular.

"Stella, whats yours?" I said sounding a bit cocky - like I wanted to. Many of the people sitting down at the benches looked shocked.

"Mason," He said cockily. This guy must be new. He didn't recognize me and I didn't recognize him. The murmurs around in the classroom stopped when he said it. He must be popular then.

"Well Mason, you can stop being so cocky because thats rude," I said, still standing against the wall. Mason started looking angry and stood up.

"Mason, sit down. Stella you can sit beside Emilie over there," The teacher said and pointed at a girl in the back. As I sat down she stared at me.

"Why are you staring?" I murmured to stop her from staring at me. Suddenly I heard Mason and another guy whisper.

"Dude, shes hot! She wasn't looking this good before she disappeared-" The guy whispered but got cut off by Mason.

"Disappeared?" Mason whispered to the guy. So Mason was kind of new here then. If he wasn't he would know who I was, everybody who I recognize seem to know who I am.

"Yeah, she kinda vanished almost two years ago. No one heard of her since. But now shes back," The guy answered and I could feel Mason looking at me.

"Why?" Mason asked. "Like why did she just disappear?"

"She was seen on her best friends party, but she stormed out and then she was gone," The guy answered. That was kind of true.

"I stormed out because your soon-to-be alpha threw a mug of soda on me," I said to Mason. "But that was not why I left though," I finished, making them both look shocked at me.

"You should stop whispering too, its rude and everyone can still hear you," I pointed out. They were still looking shocked. Everyone looked at me probably thinking "Oh my god! She just insulted the popular guy!".

"Wasn't she human?" Mason asked the guy sitting besides her. He nodded and Mason looked back at me.

"So you're all still saying that? Nah, Im not," I said as the bell rang and everybody started moving. I walked out from the room and went back to my locker. And guess what: Mason has my old one.

"Wanna switch lockers?" I asked him. He looked confused at me. Maybe it wasn't a normal question to ask here.

"Why do you want my locker?" He asked me. There are many reasons.

"Because I want my locker. They probably thought that I was dead so they gave you mine. So, I'll ask you again, do you want to switch lockers?" I asked. He shook his head. I hope that they haven't changed code.

"You know that me and my best friend knows the code to 'your' locker?" I asked. He chuckled and crossed his arms.

"And who's your best friend?" He asked. What should I answer? An magical pink cotton candy elephant? No.

"Her name is Madeleine,"

Chapter 11

"Medeleine?" He asked, shocked. "Like the alphas daughter?" He asked. Technically she's not their real daughter, but he can think so if he wants.

"Yeah. Madeleine, Maddie, Mads, Addie, the alphas daughter, whatever you wanna call her," I said whit a 'duh' tone. He scratched his neck. This boy was quite good looking with his fluffy brown hair and his attractive clothing style.

I looked up at his face. "Well then; whats her favorite food?" He asked. As if he knew, pfft.

"Pizza. And it needs to have pineapple, olives and mozzarella on it. And it needs to be home made. She likes it the most when Rachel does it, because she isn't really that good at cooking. But Rachel sure is," I said. I remember those pizzas Rachel made. The best pizza I've ever tasted.

"She always says that it is sushi..." Mason says.

"She hates sushi," I said and chuckled. Mason looked confused.

"Wait, do you know her?" I asked him and he nodded. We had been moving as we talked and now we stood next to a green wall. The paint was really old and was falling apart. There was a hole in the wall and you could see the bricks which the school was made of.

"Yeah, we've known each other for about a year or so. She was the first one who talked to me when I first moved here," He said and sat down on a bench besides the wall, waiting for the teacher to come and open the classroom.

"But then you'd know that she really isn't the alphas daughter?" I said but it sounded like a question. I sat down next to him on the old wooden bench.

"What?" So he didn't know after all. Why hasn't she told him? Well she lied about her favorite food, but thats something she does quite often. Lie about small things.

"She was found in the forest when she was about three, a week after me," I said and laid my head back at the wall. The bench sounded a bit weird when I moved.

"A week after you?" He asked me. I nodded and looked at the wall in front of us. It was green as the one behind us, but the paint on it looked new.

"They found me in the woods when I was a baby," I shrugged and let my right hand go thru my hair.

"Oh," He said. I could feel him staring at me.

"Its no biggie," I said and looked at him. "They probably had a really good reason to leave me. And Im happy without them," I said as the teacher came and opened the classroom. Me and Mason had three classes together.

We walked into the classroom and sat down next to each other. I was sitting next to the window so I could look out whenever I wanted to. Like right now.

"Which pack did you live at before?" I asked Mason. He said that he moved here a year ago and probably joined our pack too.

"The blood moon pack," Mason said. It was the pack I lived at before. But he moved only a year ago? Why didn't I recognize him?

"What? When did you move here?" I asked. He was really confused by the looks of it.

"I moved here last year in december," He said. It was august now. But then we would've met there?

"But then I must've met you? I mean I lived there for almost two years..." I said making him even mire confused. He looked quite cute though.

"Did you really move her in december? I am well known in the blood moon pack, if you moved i december you must've heard of me!" Now it was my turn to be confused.

"Wait, why are you well known there?" He asked making me face palm.

"I was the strongest and the best fighter there!" I said and he looked surprised. Almost as I just said that I was pregnant whit his child. Wait what?

"What? I thought I recognized you! You were that girl hanging out whit Sophie and her friends!" Mason said. And he was right. But why didn't I recognize him then? Maybe he wasn't around that much.

"Mason and..." The teacher said. And as everybody else, he didn't know who I was. Did I really look so different?

"Stella," I corrected him. He nodded. The rest of the lesson was super boring. I almost fell asleep. But then, to my luck, the bell rang. We all left the room to go to our lockers.

When I came to my locker Amelia stood there. She waved at me and then went in for a hug. "Its lunch, let's go to the cafeteria!" She said and took my hand to drag me there.

When we came in to the cafeteria it smelled bad. Not like: this food isn't going to taste great... More like: Oh my god it smells like puke and dead kittens!!! And thats horrible. I mean dead kittens isn't good.

"Ewww, what is that smell?" I asked Amelia. She laughed and dragged me to the food.

Rice with some kind of bead and mustard sauce. It didn't just smell bad, it looked bad. The rice didn't look like rice and the beaf was grey. The sauce was yellow, as mustard.

When we had some food on our plates we went to look for somewhere to sit. We ended up sitting on an empty table in the back of the room. But soon some other people came and sat next to us. They were probably Amelia's friend.

"Who's the new girl?" A blonde guy with green eyes said.

"Im not new, I just haven't been here for a while," I said a bit to cocky for his liking as he started looking angry.

"Jeez Andrew take a chill pill," A girl who was sitting to my right said. She had purple hair and blue eyes.

"Im Ava," She said and smiled at me. She seemed to be nice.

"Stella," I said and smiled back at her. She didn't look surprised, she was probably not going to this school when I 'disappeared'.

"So what do you mean with 'I just haven't been here for a while'?" Ava asked curiously.

"I left two years ago and came back yesterday a bit after midnight," I said and shrugged.

"Why did you leave?" Andrew asked. I glared at him but answered. "Because I was angry at everything. I mean, I had soda all over my back and this guy was really annoying and a girl at school was trying to bully me, but Im too good at comebacks so she failed. And that was annoying. My life was just to annoying and I wanted to go away for a little while, and so I did. But I was to embarrassed to go back," I answered him and he looked weirdly at me.

"So you just ran away form your family-" He started but I cut him off.

"My family left me when I was a baby, so no. I didn't leave them. I don't even know anything about them. But I left the ones who had been taking care of me all my life, yes." I made him look really embarrassed. I could almost hear his thoughts.

"Why did I even say that? She must think that Im a really bad friend. She'll probably hate me forever!!!"

"But why were your clothes covered in soda?" A girl asked. She had large blue eyes and light brown hair.

"A guy threw a mug soda on me. He's not really a casanova..." I said.

"Who?" Ava asked.

"No one really... Just the soon to be alpha of my pack," I said extremely sarcastic.

"Theo?" Amelia asked.

"Mhm," I said and everyone looked at him, he sat not that far away. He was deep in his thoughts.

"Did you know that his mate rejected him?" The girl, who I didn't know the name of, said.

"No," Everyone said, except me who said "Yeah,". Everyone looked at me.

"How did you know?" Ava asked as she put up her long hair in a pony tail.

"I was at his party," I said and looked down at the untouched food on my plate.

"What? How did you get invited?" Andrew said.

"I didn't really get invited. My 'family' did. They asked me if I wanted to go with them. But I would've got an invite if I was in town when they wrote the invites," I said and Andrew raised his dark eyebrows.

"Im his 'sisters' best friend" I said and shrugged. His eyes widened, but he was not looking at me. He was looking at something behind me. Or someone.

Chapter 12

I looked behind me, at the person Andrew was staring at. Many people looked at him. I looked up at his face.

Oh god, not him.

"What do you want?" I asked him, annoyed. He looked down at me and gave me a look that meant 'seriously?'.

"I want to talk to you," He said seriously and took a grip around my right arm. I could feel sparks where his hand touched my arm. It was nice sparks though.

"Ugh, fine!" I said and followed him out from the cafeteria. He still wouldn't release my arm from his grip even though I tried pulling his hand away from my arm.

We went trough some corridors and trough a door. Suddenly I felt fresh air in my lungs, we were outside. He released the grip a bit and dragged me with him to a tree.

"Why?" He asked sadly as he let go of my arm. I felt empty when the sparks disappeared.

"What?" I responded and looked up at his blue eyes. They were quite cool. Light blue around the pupil and darker on the outside of the iris. In the left eye you could see a tiny bit of brown near the pupil. My brown eyes weren't near as beautiful - wait what? Did I just call his eyes beautiful?

"Why did you reject me?" He asked as he looked into my eyes, sending chills down my spine. I looked away.

There were many reasons. Mainly because he was just an annoying piece of shit. But also because he was an alpha and I didn't want to be a luna. They have to care about everyone in the pack. Especially the children. And theres the problem: I hate children. They are screaming, annoying, eating boogers, discussing and just things I don't want to be around.

I just simply shrugged as an answer. He didn't seam so impressed by my answer.

"You don't know?" He asked whit a tiny bit of anger in his voice. "You just did it?" He asked as he punched the tree, making lots of leaves fall off and a branch fall on the other side of the tree.

"There are many reasons," I said quietly, a bit scared that he would punch me the next time. But he wont, Im his mate. You don't really punch your mate.

"Give me one," He said and I shook my head making him even more angry. "Say them all then," He said quite high making me even more scared. But I still shook my head. I didn't want to tell him.

"Why not?" He said sounding really frustrated. I would be too if I was in his situation.

"I don't want to," I said lowly and looked down at the grass below my feet. If I wouldn't have had shoes on right now, the grass would've tickled my toes.

"Well then write a note. And give it to me," He said and walked away. A note?

The rest of the day went super slow and I had a headache. Theo's words were still circling in my head. "Then write a note".

I walked to my locker and looked down at my feet. And what happens when you don't look up? You bump in to someone. And thats exactly what I did.

"Sorry," I murmured and started to walk to my locker once again, but got stopped by a hand holding my arm.

"What?" I asked and looked up at the guys face. It was a face I didn't recognize at all.

"I was about to insult you, but wow you're really pretty," The guy said making me blush. He wasn't that bad looking with his brown eyes and dark hair.

"Thank you," I said and smiled at him. He smiled back at me and introduced himself as Anthony and I told him that my name was Stella.

'He's cute, but he's not our mate!' Luceat told me. I already knew that. He was really cute. And I knew that he wasn't our mate. But we rejected our mate.

'No! You rejected him!' Luceat growled at me. Okey, I did.

"Bye," I told him as he was going right where I was going left. "Bye," He responded and walked to his locker as I walked to mine.

I opened it and took my jacket and backpack and put them on. The black helmet I held in my hand as I locked the locker and went to the schools parking lot.

I put on the helmet and drove away home on the motorcycle. The words came back in my head. "Then write a note". And that is what I will do.

When I came home no one was there. I went straight up to my room and started to write the letter.

"The note you wanted.

There are many reasons why I would reject you. You wanted a note on them, so here I go...

We can begin with how much I hate you." No that wasn't good. I threw the note in the trashcan underneath my table and started writing a new one. After several notes, which I threw away because they were bad, I had one to give him.

"Dear Theo, no, just Theo. This is that note you wanted me to write. I have never liked you in some special way. You've only been 'Maddie's annoying little brother' for me. And that is what you'll stay as. I think that the Moon Goddess have made a big mistake. Why would you be my mate? You are an alphas first born, you'll be an alpha one day. And I wont be your luna. I wasn't made to be one. I hate people, and children. I could never help you run a pack as a luna. That would just not be my thing. And I just can't see you and me together in any way possible. We're not going to work. I've always been a little bit mad on you. When I was little it was because you would tear mine and Maddie's toys apart and now because you're you. And I'm not even ready for a relationship yet. And I have been seeing myself as a single lady all my life. I've always wanted to be known as 'the lady who never found her mate, but is happy anyways'. Unfortunately that wont be my story.

I hope you understand."

I knocked on Theo and Maddie's house door with the note folded in my hand. It didn't take long until the door was opened. Maddie's tired face met mine and she smiled.

"Uhm, I have some notes Theo wanted for the homework..." I said and showed her the note. She nodded and shouted at Theo to come down. When he saw me at the door he first looked a bit confused, but when I showed him the note he took it fast and rushed up to his room.

"Well, you look like you need some sleep. So I'll go now. Bye!" I said and gave Maddie a hug and chuckled. Then I left.

I wonder what Theo will think when he reads the note.

My phone was in my pocket. I swiftly took it up and texted Theo.

"Burn it after you've read it."

Chapter 13

Saturday.

What to do?

Maybe I should be healthy and go out and run for an hour or so. Or I'll just stay in bed.

Even though the second choice was tempting, I did go out for a run. Not for an hour though. Half an hour. Right now I had stopped at a café and am currently sipping on a glass of juice. I was listening to everyones conversations around me.

"What are you gonna do? He doesn't like kids" A man said to a woman, who was sitting on the other side of the table of him. She looked really nervous.

"But he's my fiance..." The woman began, but didn't finish. She was probably pregnant with some guys kid, and the guy hated kids. Her eyes were pointing down at something on her lap as she sighed heavily.

"I know. But still; He hates children. He would get super angry if he heard that you were pregnant!" The man said. Humans are quite weird. I don't understand why the man who wants to spend his whole life with her would get angry if she was pregnant. Isn't it every mans dream to get kids? Or its just the man who's speaking to her who is a bit stupid.

"Charles, even though you think he will get mad, he wont. I know him," The woman said as she angrily put on her coat and stormed out from the café. Charles, if that was his name, just looked like he was in his own thoughts.

When I had no juice left in the glass I left the café to walk home. Outside the sun was shining upon the sky. There were a couple of clouds on the blue heaven and the wind was stroking my bare legs and arms.

It was still august and I was running in a pair of shorts and a t-shirt with a sports bra underneath it. Otherwise I would sweat like a pig, and thats something I'd rather not do. Even though I'm part wolf, and shouldn't really sweat that much, for some reason I do.

As I put up my hair in a ponytail I could sense an familiar aroma. Mint and a tiny bit of pizza. I looked around, to find where it came from. Or more exactly, where he was. As my brown eyes were looking around they met a pair of blue ones. I knew exactly who owned those. Theo.

We stared at each other for a bit, until I realized what I was doing. I looked at the ground before sprinting off. When I was so far away from him I stopped. Only to see a forest. Maybe my wolf wants to run for a bit too?

'Yes, yes, yes, yes, yes, yes!' Luceat said. She was really excited because I rarely shifted into my wolf. I had only done it a couple of times before. Once when I was seven and two more times when I was far away in the woods.

Slowly I walked longer and longer into the forest. This made me feel at home, all the birds chirping, the beautiful trees and their leaves who soon will be changing colors and fall off. The green grass on the ground and all the flowers with their different colors. All this. It made me feel calm.

I sat down for a bit. Just listening to the birds melody and the wind brushing trough the leaves. After a little while I got up and looked around. When I didn't see anybody around I took off my clothes and changed into my wolf. I took up the clothes in my mouth and ran around in the forest. When I didn't feel like running anymore, I changed back and put on my clothes. Slowly I started walking out from the forest.

I swiftly turned around when I heard a stick break. In front of me was a wolf. It had typical wolf colours; grey with a bit of blackish. One of the eyes was brown and the other one was blue. It looked a but like an husky, but I knew that it was a wolf.

"Change," I said to the wolf when I saw the clothes it had in its mouth. The wolf went behind a big tree and changed into a human. It was a boy, he looked to be about fourteen, and he wasn't from my pack.

"Which pack are you from?" I asked the boy. He bit his lip and sat down on a big stone.

"None," He said and looked up at me. I could tell that he was really nervous by the way he looked at me.

"Rogue..." I murmured and looked down. I've met rogues before, but not on my own. I know that they are really dangerous.

"What are you doing here?" I asked him. He put his hands in his hair and then down at the stone. I could hear him sigh lowly.

"Trying to join a pack..." He murmured, but I heard it. I nodded and looked at the boy. He was quite muscular. I assume he's a good fighter too.

"Perhaps you can join mine," I said and he smiled, showing his teeth. "We can go there now," I said and he stood up. We started to walk. "And we'll have to hope that the alphas son isn't there," I murmured quietly.

"Why?" He asked. So he has really good hearing too. Well, all shifters has. But he could hear me whisper as quiet as a mouse.

"What?" I asked. He looked at me as if I said that 83 + 1 was 4, or something like that.

"Why should we hope that the alphas son isn't there?" He asked and stopped, probably thinking something terrible would happen if Theo was there.

"Can you keep secrets?" No one knew that I was Theo's mate. Not even Maddie. Well, Theo did, and I. I felt weird about me knowing that he was my mate, I wasn't supposed to feel the sparks or the attraction for him until I was eighteen. This is making my mind go all fuzzy...

"Yeah, why?"

"The alphas son, Theo, is my mate. But I rejected him. Nobody knows that Im his mate, and I want to keep it that way," I said and he nodded. The rest of the walk was fun. The boy had told me that his name was Joey and that he in fact was fourteen.

"Heres the pack house," I said and we walked in. Small growls were heard from the living room. Probably because Joey was a rouge.

"Chill," I shouted to them as we walked past. When we were outside of the alphas office, I told Joey to knock on the door.

"Come in," I heard Jaxon say and I opened the door. Jaxon was still looking angry, has he been angry since Theo's party?

"This is Joey. He wants to join our pack," Jaxon looked at Joey and then back at me.

"No," Jaxon simply said and looked back at his papers.

"No? Jaxon, look at these mussels," I said and held up Joeys arm. "Don't we need new warriors? Plus; Joey knows how to fight rouges!" I said. Now it was my turn to get angry.

"We don't have anywhere for him to live, and he's a rouge," Jaxon said, still looking down at his papers.

"Well then... I'm going back to the blood moons for a week or so. Bye!" The blood moons would never say no to a good fighter.

"You can't just leave like that!" Jaxon said and growled lowly at me. I growled back at him and turned around.

"Yes I can, bye!" I said and dragged Joey with me.

"We're going to the blood moon's. They will accept you there. Plus; theres some super nice people there, not like these," I said and started walking in the direction of my house.

"Where are we going?" Joey asked me in confusion. He probably didn't get anything and was just following me because he didn't know how to find anything around here.

"To my house to get my motorbike, then we're going to the blood moon pack," I said and turned left. Joey followed every step I took. Even though the sun was about to set in half an hour or so, I was going there to get this boy a pack.

Chapter 14

"Travis wheres your helmet?!" I screamed as I came in to the house. The stairs creaked and soon Travis stood in front of me and Joey. He quickly glanced at Joey, and then looked at me.

"Who's he?" Travis asked and pointed at the boy at my right. Travis probably thought that Joey was my boyfriend or something like that. And I could imagine his thoughts of me going away again; but with a boy! Honestly, I'd never do that.

"This is Joey. Joey this is Travis," I said and introduced them to each other."Jaxon didn't want Joey to join our pack, so Im going to get him a pack. I'll be back tomorrow. So, wheres your helmet?" Travis looked a bit confused. I would be too, if I was him. Travis shook his head.

"You ain't going anywhere..." Travis said. I groaned and punched the wall to get the anger off of me. But of course; the wall broke. Now we have a hole in the middle of the wall. Great!

"C'mon. Travis, Joey needs to get a pack. And I know the perfect one for him!" I said and put my arm around Joey's shoulders. Travis shook his head once again.

"Then I'll ask Willow," I said and went to the living room. And as I thought, Willow was sitting watching TV. She was probably watching some kind of cooking program.

"Hey Stella..." She began but shut her mouth as she saw Joey. "Who is he?" She asked, looking at Joey.

"Joey, this is Joey. He needs a pack and Jaxon wont let him join ours, and I got the perfect one for him. But Travis wont let him borrow his helmet," I said and Willow gave him a sad smile.

"Which pack?" Willow asked me, still looking at Joey.

"The one I was at..." I murmured, but made sure that she heard. I looked down at my feet and bit the inside of my chin.

"I can drive you there," She looked at me and shut off the TV.

"Bu-"

"No, I'll drive you there. Which pack?" She said and started walking to the hall. Joey and I followed her.

"The blood moon's" I said. Se nodded and took her car keys and we went out to the car.

It was quite cold outside now and it was starting to get dark. I sat down in the back of the car, next to Joey.

Willow started driving when we had put on our seat belts. Great, a two hour drive with my mom and Joey.

"So, Joey, how old are you?" Willow asked, obviously curious about this boy.

"Fourteen," He said and looked out the window. I did so too. There where trees on both sides of the car.

"Have you been rouge all your life?" Willow asked. She was a very curious woman. Sometimes she asked super irrelevant questions and realizing what she asked when the person looks sad or angry.

"Yep, but I don't want to anymore," He said and tilted his head to look down at his feet. I could see Willow nodding in the corner of my eye.

"How did you and Stella meet?" Willow asked him as she focused at the road.

"I was running in the forest and was lost. Then I saw her and decided to follow her because she looked like she knew the way out, then she heard me and we started talking. She said I could join her pack, but that didn't work..." He said.

"Are we there yet?" I asked Willow, even though I knew that we'll have to drive for about an hour more to get there.

"No. In about an hour or so," Willow said, still looking at the road. But that was good, I really don't want to crash.

My eyelids felt heavy, really heavy. I closed them.

"Maddie?" I asked a little brown haired girl who stood in a pink princess dress in front of me.

"Yeah?" The little girl said and sat down in front of me.

"We're besties right?" I asked and she giggled and nodded. I smiled. My little hands went into hers.

"And besties tell each other everything right?" She nodded as an answer to my question.

"I'll tell you all my secrets, no matter what!" She said, super seriously.

"And I'll tell you mine." I said and put my little hand over my heart. She mimicked me and her other hand slipped out of mine.

"I HAVE A CRUSH ON TIMMIE!" She shouted and which made me giggle.

"Stella we're here!" Joey said as he slapped me to wake me up.

"Chill, Im awake!" I said and took off my seat belt and went out of the car.

"Follow me," I said to both Joey and Willow. Then I ran into the building.

"Hello?!" I shouted and I heard someone scream, followed by some laughs. We followed the sounds and came into the living room.

"Stella!" Sophie jumped onto me, almost making me fall. Soon I was in the middle of a group hug.

"What are you doing here?" Max, a really cute guy, said. They all let go off me and then they looked at Joey and Willow.

"Joey here needs a pack," I said pointing towards Joey. He smiled at them and they nodded.

"Our stupid alpha wouldn't let him join our pack, so I immediately thought of you. Plus that I wanted to meet y'all," I said.

"And she?" Max asked, pointing towards Willow.

"Thats Willow. You guys know who she is," I said and shrugged. I had told them all about my family. Every thing from what their names were, to what they used to eat for breakfast. I had told them about how girlish Travis were, but how he still were 100% guy-ish. I had told them about Willows strawberry smell and how she got fixed in the morning. Connor, oh boy. I had told them about his car obsession, how loving he was to his son and that he wore socks in his sandals.

Max nodded, making his brown fluffy hair wiggle. He was much longer than me, almost 15 cm. Unfortunately he made fun out of me for being so "short". I wasn't that short, I was about 176 cm long. Compared to Sophia's 166 cm, that was quite long.

"Can someone take Joey to the alpha and ask if he can join the pack?" I asked, mostly towards Tanya. Tanya was the alphas daughter and she was the only one he really cared for, besides his mate. Tanya nodded and took Joey with her to her dads office.

"Are we sleeping here?" I asked Willow, but she shook her head. I knew that she didn't like sleeping at somewhere else than at home.

"Alright, we'll go now. I'll pay a visit soon, I promise!" I said and hugged all my friends once again. Although I really wanted to stay, I really wanted to sleep at home.

"Oh, and guys, be nice to Joey! Bye!" I said and walked out with Willow. I heard them all say a "bye" before we left.

Chapter 15

I was woken up by a screaming Travis sitting on my bed. Did he want to make me deaf?

"What the hell are you doing?" I asked him as I sat up. He looked at me and a bright smile grew on his face when he saw that I was awake.

"We're gonna go and buy food!" He shouted. What was he doing? He rarely screams or makes high noices.

"Why the hell are you screaming? Are you on drugs?" I asked him. He didn't really look like he was on drugs, but he kind of acted like he was. He simply chuckled as an answer and shook his head.

"No, I just wanted to wake you up. Let's go to the store!" He said and dragged me down on the floor.

"Ow!" I shouted as my hip hit the wooden floor. Travis surely acted weird today. He hasn't been like this since we were small, or since the day he met his mate.

"Oh shit sorry!" He said when he noticed that I got hurt. This was more like the normal Travis. My hand landed on my sore hip.

"I'll go down. Be in the living room in half an hour," He said and ran downstairs. What the heck is wrong with him today?

I didn't want to shower today, at least not in the morning. I was simply too tired. So I just put on a pair of black jeans and a white t-shirt. As it was getting colder outside I forced myself to put on an light grey cardigan too.

Swiftly I ran down the creaking stairs and shouted at Travis, telling him that I was done to go. We both put on our shoes and went out.

"Wieee!" Travis said as he jumped down the stairs. Okay, something is terribly wrong.

"Travis? Are you okay?" I asked him seriously. He just laughed and dragged his hand trough his short light brown hair.

"Travis why are you acting so weird?" I was quite worried about him. He never acted like this. Was it something he had eaten?

"I asked Dawn if she would marry me; and she said yes!" Travis said with tears in his eyes as he clapped his hand.

"Oh my god Travis! When? Where?" I had so many questions, but right now I was so happy for him. And that made me think about Theo...How I just selfishly left him without even getting to know him.

"Yesterday, when you and mom had left. I took her a bit into the forest and we were looking up at the stars and I asked her," He said while a tear was rolling down his cheek.

"Can I be your best man? But like your best woman instead?" He chuckled at my thought. Did it really sound that weird?

"Yeah, sure," He said as we were walking down the road, to the shop. Travis and Dawn was the cutest couple ever. They both had the best humor ever and they had the same music taste. What if Theo has the same music taste as me... Wait what? Why was I thinking about him so much? I could even smell that mint sent of his. Ugh!

"Look, Theo's over there!" Travis said and looked at Theo who was talking to his friends. So I wasn't imagining his sent... Thats good; I thought I was going crazy.

"And we're going this way," I said and tried to go the opposite way of where Theo was. He is the last person I want to talk to right now.

"No, let's go and talk to him. He has had a rough time, now when his mate has rejected him and all..." Travis said and I shook my head. No way Im going over thereto talk to him.

Suddenly I felt like I was flying. But turns out, Travis had put me over his shoulder and was now walking over to Theo. Fortunately my face was on Travis's back, so I didn't have to look at him.

"Hey," Travis said as he stopped. Most girls would've kicked him and punched him and made him let go of them. But right now it would be very awkward if he did so.

And guess what, he let me down.

"Bye," I said without looking at Theo and his friends and started walking away. But my life was a pain in the ass, so Travis stopped me.

"No," Travis said and I groaned. He pulled me towards him, and I was soon standing against his chest.

"Anyways, Hi," Travis smiled to his friends. Yes, Theo and Travis were both very good friends.

"Hi," Theo said, but he was clearly looking at me. I growled lowly at him, so he would stop staring. Instead Travis hit me on my arm.

"Everybody keeps staring at me, its annoying. Okey?" I said to them both. Theo clearly got a bit angry. Travis just chuckled, thinking it sounded fun for some reason.

"What have you been doing lately?" Travis asked the guys who was standing in front of us.

"Training," A muscular guy said. He was slightly more muscular than the others. In this town; everybody was muscular. It was quite annoying.

"Dealing with an angry dad who has been asking a lot of questions," Theo said, looking at me in the corner of his eye. I hid a smile and leaned against Travis.

'You owe me for not telling him anything' It was the first time someone who wasn't Maddie mind-linked me. Everybody else wasn't able to. We've tried for years, but nobody besides Maddie could min-link me.

"Travis," I said with my eyes widened. He understood that it was something important and nodded.

"He just mind-linked me," I whispered, really confused. This was scary. Theo and his friends looked more confused.

"How?" Travis asked Theo. "How were you able to do that?" Travis put both his hands on Theo's shoulders shaking him.

"What?" Theo sounded really nervous, but a bit confused. He looked at me and his eyebrows crashed together.

"You just mind-linked her!" Travis shook Theo. He obviously didn't know about how nobody could mind-link me.

"Yeah?" Theo asked and I could tell how nervous he was. It was actually a bit funny to watch.

"Nobody besides Maddie can, or could, do that!" Travis said and looked at me. I was just as confused as everybody else.

"So thats why everybody think shes human," The muscular guy said. I nodded.

'How the heck...' I mind-linked to Theo. He didn't answer. Travis was dragging him somewhere.

"What are you doing Travis?" I asked him and ran to him. He quickly looked at me, but his focus went back to Theo and he looked like he was in deep thoughts.

"Taking you two to the pack doctor" He said as he grabbed my wrist and dragged me along.

"What, no!" Theo said and tried to get out from Travis grip but he just tightened it.

When we were right outside the pack doctors house both me and Theo tried breaking out from Travis's grip, but that didn't work at all. Instead he dragged us into the house and straight to the pack doctors office. She opened the door and made us sit in uncomfortable chairs as she talked.

"We must examine this," Was the only thing I heard before I stopped listening.

'Im gonna run out the door in ten seconds or so.' Theo mind-linked me. I nodded and counted down.

10, 9, 8, 6, 7. Wait I screwed up. Thats not how it goes!

Before I could correct myself Theo stood up and went to run to the door. But he didn't succeed. Travis was too fast, he grabbed Theo's arm and forced him to sit down again.

"We're going to go to this other room," The pack doctor said. I couldn't remember her name, and I didn't bother to ask.

We went out in the corridor again and walked for a bit until we came to a room. The doctor opened the door and we went into the room. There was one of those hospital beds in the middle of the room. It had super ugly green bedsheets and the mattress was probably hard as a stone.

"You two can sit down on the bed," The woman said. Theo and I sat as far away from each other as we possibly could on the uncomfortable bed.

"And you can go out in the corridor and wait," The woman said to Travis.

"Bu-"

"Theres some chairs there," The woman said and pushed Travis out from the room. Then she close the door and locked it. I noticed that she were quite young, maybe in her twenties.

"So you are mates, huh?" She asked, looking a bit too over excited. I rolled my eyes at the question. In the corner of my eye I could see Theo slowly nodding. I growled at him, making him stop.

"Hm," The woman said and I looked back at her. "I heard that you rejected him," She said pointing towards me. I shrugged and laid back on the bed.

"But it looks like you still like each other," She said making me shake my head. Theo was just looking at me.

"You should give him a chance," The woman said and I could feel Theo getting happy.

"Anyways, you two can mind-link because your mates, I'll leave you now. You can leave when you want to," She said and left the room.

"What did she say?" Travis sais as he came into the room and sat down in a chair in the corner of the room.

"It was something about him having alpha blood or something," I shrugged. My lies wasn't usually that great but this one seemed to work.

"Oh, alright. Uhm, I need to go. Dawn called and said-" Travis said but I cut him off.

"Yeah, we get it," I said and watched him walk out. He gave us a "bye" before he left.

It was quite awkward just sitting silently in a room... With my mate. And I knew that he was staring at me.

"Stop staring, its rude," I said to stop him from staring at me. But that was unsuccessful.

"But your so beautiful... I can't," He said. Did he really? Why was I blushing?

Chapter 16

The past 15 minutes I've been staring into his eyes. It wasn't awkward at all, I just felt peaceful. But when we both heard footsteps in the corridor our eyes flew to the door. It sounded like there was about three people out there, walking towards this room. Suddenly, a man stood in the doorframe. It was Jaxon.

"Theo... And Stella?" He was probably a bit surprised that I was here. Perhaps we should be surprised too. He looked around the room, as Theo and I did when we came here.

"What are you doing here?" Jaxon asked. I would like to ask him that same question. I mean, why were he here? Did he even know that Theo was here?

"I was able to mind-link her so Travis dragged us here and a doctor came, we didn't really listen to her..." Theo explained and Jaxon nodded. Jaxon already knew that nobody could mind-link me, besides Maddie. I looked at Theo, he was a bit nervous.

"What are you doing here?" Theo asked his father. Jaxon sat down in the chair in the corner and looked back at his son. I hope that I wont be in the middle of some family drama by sitting here right now.

"I heard that you were here, so I came to look if you were hurt," Jaxon said. It was nice that he cared about his son. Theo nodded slowly as I laid down on the bed again. I looked up at the roof, it was white but quite dirty.

"But you weren't, so we can go home now," Jaxon said and stood up. For some reason I didn't want Theo to leave, but it would be suspicious if he didn't want to.

'Bye' I mind-linked him. He jumped off of the bed and went out if the room with his dad.

'See you later...' Theo mind-linked me.

'What? No. Nope, no, no, no, no, no, no' I responded and then went out in the corridor myself. I slowly walked trough them until I came to the reception. The door opened by itself and I walked out into the rain. I breathed out. A little cloud appeared in front of my mouth, but disappeared the second after.

If I had a phone, I would listen to some depressive music right now. I had one, before I left. But I left it with everything else. That was my first phone, and hopefully last. Phones wasn't things that I really liked. They were just good to have.

Emergency? Call help, on your phone.

Need to talk to someone who is far, far away? Call them!

That was what a phone was to me. But of course you can use them to look at when you don't want to talk to somebody or avoid them.

I kicked a stone as I walked. Theo came to my thoughts, how could he even be my mate? And how could I feel it? I mean, I'd had gotten my mate, or found, him/her when I turn eighteen. And I shouldn't feel the sparks or anything before that... Life's strange. Especially for me.

'Why do you have to be so negative by everything?' Luceat asked. She hadn't spoken for a while, but I was glad that she was back.

'Its the rain,' I answered. Rain always got me a bit depressed. Maybe because the rain brings depressing colors: grey, other shades of grey, more shades of gray.

Why couldn't they record 50 shades of grey in the rain. Or just film the sky. That would be much nicer, so very much nicer than what they filmed.

I bumped into something hard, which made me stop thinking about whatever I was thinking about.

"Ouch!" Great, I've bumped into a guy.

"Sorry," I murmured. He glared at me, as if we knew each other and we were enemies.

"Why did you just walk into me? That super rude, ugh!" The guy complained. He acted just like someone I knew... Oh yeah, myself.

"Well, you kinda walked into me too. You could've moved to the left or right, but you decided to walk right into me," I said and shrugged. His face turned red, but just slightly.

"No, you could've!" He said cockily, probably because he didn't have any good comebacks in mind.

"No, because I was too deep in my thought," I said to him calmly, just to piss him off more.

"Same," He said. What the hell? We're not on some kind of social media where you comment "same" to quotes or pictures. This is real life, not social medias.

He blushed when he saw me in confusion. "Well, bye!" I said and walked away. He didn't answer. Rude.

'To be honest, you're kind of the rude one... Always negative, always selfish, always grumpy-' I cut her off. That was enough negative things for a day... Said to me.

Although I can be nice, I use not to. It was just something I was used to; being rude.

'CAN THEO MIND-LINK YOU?!? WHY DIDN'T YOU TELL ME?!?!?' Maddie suddenly screamed trough the mind-link. Ouch! My ears! My ears? When you mind-link you hear it in your head, not ears! Ugh, why do I have to be so stupid?

'Yay! Now we can have group conversations!' Maddie cheered. She've always been excited about this day. She always had hope for it to come. I stopped caring a few years ago. Why would anyone be able to mind-link me? The only one I really wanted to mind-link was Maddie.

'No-' I tried, but she didn't listen. When I heard Theo's confused voice in the mind-link I cut them off. I'd rather talk to Luceat all day than talk to Maddie and Theo in the mind-link.

Something felt like they were quite annoying.

I sighed out in the open air.

The rain had stopped and the clouds were starting to clear up. When I saw the light blue sky I smiled. But that smile soon faded when I heard Luceat whimper.

'Something... Isn't right...' Luceat was very nervous, which she rarely was. My heart started to beat like crazy and my steps were quicker.

'Luceat? Whats wrong?' She obviously didn't know, but I had to ask.

She didn't answer, making me more nervous. Whatever's happening - it isn't good, at all.

Chapter 17

S lowly I closed the door to the house. The low murmurs from the living room stopped as soon as I stepped into the house.

Oh god, this is creepy. My heart is going to stop. I don't feel well.

"Stella?" The voice, who I would assume is Willow's, said nervously. What have I done now?

"Yeah?" I tried to hold my voice stable, but with this creepy feeling over me I couldn't really.

"Can you come over here?" Connor, Willow's man, said. This was making me even more nervous if it possibly could.

Slowly I made my way into the living room. As I came in, everyone stared at me.

In there Willow and Connor, who I had heard, sat. Also Travis and... Jaxon?

I looked at Willow and Connor with my eyebrows tied together. They both gave me a half hearted smile and then looked at Jaxon. I looked at him too.

"What are you doing here?" I asked him lowly. My voice still sounded nervous and in the bottom of my stomach I could feel that something was wrong.

He smirked. "You see, a girl rejected her mate; my son, this week."

"And..?" I said, but I knew where he was going with this.

"I've heard that you're this girl." Jaxon said.

"And who've told you that?" I asked, raising my voice slightly.

"Thats not important. The thing thats important is that you've betrayed your pack." Jaxon said, I could tell that he's angry. To my relief, he wasn't as angry as he was on Theo's party. So I won't get killed today then? Good.

"You, Stella Adams, is now banned from the Paper Moon pack and territory - forever." Jaxon said and glared at me.

"Bu-"

"Pack your stuff and leave!" He said in his alpha tone. I shyly nodded and ran upstairs, to my already packed bags. Ever since I came back, just a few days ago, I hadn't packed anything up. You don't really know when you're gonna be going again, huh? So why hurry and pack up everything when you don't know if you will stay a day or a week? Thats kind of pointless, according to me that is.

After closing the bags I ran downstairs and took my helmet. I didn't even bother to hug my "family" and say goodbye, they didn't even care about me being banned. Their faces were blank, not showing any emotions at all.

'Karma' Luceat chuckled. Yeah, she was right. Bad karma.

I can't remember for how long I drove, longer than to the Blood Moon pack atleast. Because I certainly didn't stop there.

The motorbike coughed, telling me the gas was out. I jumped off it and started leading it. Right now, I just wanted to find somewhere to sleep.

"Need help?" I stiffed when I heard the voice. Clearly, there was a guy behind me. He was a werewolf, and I was one hundred precent sure of that. I was probably smelling gasoline, from the bike, and therefor he couldn't know if I was a human or not.

Slowly I turned around, seeing a guy who looked to be around seventeen. As usual, like everyone with werewolf traits, he looked good.

"Maybe," I said and took off my helmet so he could hear, and see, me.

He walked to the motorcycle and took it from me. I didn't mind, he wouldn't be able to drive away with it anyway.

"So, where are you going? And why are you out in the forest in the middle of the night?" He asked and looked down at me. Why did I have to be so short? I mean, he can easily just spit in my face right now.

"Hm, I don't know where I'm going and I'm out in the forest... Uhm, I'm kind of searching for somewhere to stay..." I said and he nodded understandingly.

"I'm Shaun by the way." He smiled at me.

"Stella." I smiled back at him.

"Uhm, I live over there," Shaun said and pointed to his right. "In my pa- I mean family's house." So he couldn't sense that I was like him then.

"In your pack house." I corrected him and he looked confused. Slowly he figured that I was a werewolf too, but my scent was covered by the gasoline smell.

"Thank God! I hate being with humans, they're so hard to talk to!" He said and smiled at me happily. Yeah, I have to agree on that. Humans are weird.

We walked over to his pack house. Shaun had told me that his dad was the packs third in command and that his packs name was Shadow Woods.

'That sounds so much better than Paper Moon!' Luceat told me, and I agreed. Whoever came up with 'Paper Moon' was very uncreative.

We parked my motorcycle outside of the pack house. Fortunately, most people was asleep. Being stared at isn't something that I like.

We walked into the pack house. When the warmth of the house hit me, I realized how could I really was. Even though I am a werewolf, and shouldn't be freezing so easily, I was very could.

The pack house itself was very cosy, but still modern. I liked it.

We were soon standing in front of a big wooden door. "Knock." Shaun murmured to me, and so I did.

"Enter" A dark voice said. Shaun opened the door and stepped in, with me in the lead.

"Shaun?" The man, who probably was the alpha, sounded surprised. "What brings you here, in the middle of the night?" The alpha-guy asked Shaun. He probably didn't realize that I stood here, or he choose not to look at me.

"I was out for a walk, you see. And then I found Stella," He said, turning to me. The alpha glanced at me, but looked back at Shaun quickly to hear what he had to say.

"She basically needs a new pack." Shaun said. The alpha looked at me.

"And why do you need a new one?" The alpha said.

"I got kicked out of mine." I said lowly. The alpha got curious.

"And why were kicked out?" He said, playing with a pen between his fingers.

"Betrayal." I said lowly and shrugged.

"Which kind?" The alpha asked. Shaun looked curious too.

"I rejected the soon-to-be alpha as my mate..." I murmured, but made sure that the alpha could hear.

He nodded slowly. "I think you should get some rest, and tell me more tomorrow." The alpha said and looked at Shaund. They were probably mind-linking.

Shaun led me to a room. It kind of looked like a hotel room of some sort, but I'm glad that they had a nice room for me to stay in.

"Thanks." I told him and gave him a quick hug before he left. The bags, which still both were placed on my back, I laid down on the bed. Once I had found my pajamas, a yellow t-shirt and a pair of blue sleeping shorts, I put it on. I looked a bit like the Swedish flag, or the Ukrainian one. Yellow and blue.

I lifted down the bags and laid down on the bed. What a long day.

Chapter 18

Theo's POV

I sat in my dads car as he drove us home. Staring out the window I saw how the clouds started to clear up a little bit from the previous rain. The birds were out flying again, searching for food. You could hear them chirp sometimes, and especially if you were like me - a werewolf.

"I think I've found that girl." My dad said, staring at the road in front of the car. He was still angry for what happened at my party, but I wasn't. I have not been that angry at her, I mean she had her reasons. We're only fifteen after all.

"Mhm?" I muttered, not really interested in what he had to say. He was probably suspecting a poor girl from the pack, who he's been seeing me being with like one time or two.

"So when I have dropped you off, I will be going to hers." He said and I nodded, but still not feeling so good about this. My stomach had a nervous feeling in the bottom of it. I didn't know why though, Stella wasn't someone who he would suspect, right?

The car stopped, making me look out the front window. There I saw the pack house, not the Alpha house. Why did he stop here?

"I'll drop you off here, see you later Theo." He said and I nodded as I took off the seat belt. Slowly I opened the car door and went out.

"Theo!" Someone shouted. I closed the car door and looked around. "Over here!" I saw my best friend, Aden, stand near the forest to the right of the pack house.

"Why you looking all nervous, man?" He asked me. Honestly, I didn't really know. Something isn't right, thats all I know.

I shrugged and answered him. "Don't know. Something isn't right..." He gave me a smile.

"Wanna go for a run?" He asked, probably because he was planning to run right now. I nodded and we went behind some trees and took our clothes off. Then we shifted. When we were on our paws we took our clothes in out mouths.

Aden's wolf was brown and he had bright blue eyes. His wolf wasn't as big as mine, but it wasn't small. He was going to be my beta, and he was the son of my dads beta, making his wolf bigger than everybody else's - except from the Alphas, like me.

My wolf was grey with a couple of black streaks in its fur. My eyes were green, very green. If you looked at them really close you could see some brown specks in the left one.

As we started running I felt free. I loved everything about this. The wind running trough my fur, the fresh air, running - I love running in general.

When I was running as fast as I could, I had to stop. Something is very wrong. I can just... Feel it.

'Whats up, dude? Why did you stop running?' Aden mind-linked me. He was confused. I was just standing still.

'Stella...' My wolf, Geo, howled. Is she hurt? Is she okey?

'We must check if she's okey!' My wolf told me. I nodded and slowly turned around. Faster than ever before, I ran to her house with a really confused friend trailing behind me.

The door was open and my dads car was standing in their front yard. I made my way into the house, still in wolf form.

My dad was sitting in the living room with her family. He smiled at me.

'Where's she?' I asked him trough the mind-link. His smile grew bigger and he looked really happy with something.

A high growl left my mouth and his smile faded. 'Where. Is. She?' I asked once again, angrily as I glared at him.

"I banned her from our territory." He said, with a evil smile creeping up upon his lips. I growled at him once again before leaving.

Stella's family didn't even look sad. What was wrong with them? Don't they have emotions? Their daughter was banned, their goddamn daughter! And Travis, one of my good friends, he just had a blank expression on his face. He always said that they were really close, before she left. He was always so sad after she left, but he had hope in her coming back. And now, when she's banned from our packs territory he wasn't even a little bit sad?

I ran into the forest and didn't stop until I was a few meters from the border. He can't just ban her! He, he just can't!

'Maddie...' Someone has to tell her about this. Last time Stella left, Maddie stopped talking, eating and having hope in life. She had just about started to communicate with everybody besides me, her mate and my parents when Stella came back. And now shes banned...

'Yeah? What is it lil' bro?' She asked happily. Oh god, I hope that Im not about to ruin her day.

'Dad banned Stella from our territory...' I told her. She went quiet for a long time until she spoke again. 'Why?' Her voice was broken and it sounded as she was about to cry anytime now.

I waited for a bit until I answered. 'She was my mate...' I said quietly, but high enough for her to hear. She gasped and mumbled small things that I couldn't hear.

'Why didn't she tell- why didn't you tell me?' She asked me. I didn't know. Maybe I thought that Stella would've told her?

I cut Maddie off. She will get to know eventually. I mean, dad will force me to tell everyone in the pack, probably really soon too.

Looking up at the darkening sky, I howled loudly.

My mate is gone, she will never come back. I will never see that beautiful smile of hers, that astonishing body she has and I will never breathe in her wonderful scent again. Never.

I howled again, in pain. From far away I could hear others howl in sympathy. But they don't know why I, their future alpha, was howling in pain. Unfortunately, they will, soon.

Chapter 19

"Madeleine!" A woman's voice shouted. She sounded irritated.

The little girl who sat in front of me groaned. "What?"

"Stop screaming!" The woman screamed. Madeleine, which was the girls name, giggled at me.

"No, mommy, we're not screaming at all!" Madeleine shouted back at the woman. She giggled once again, I giggled back at her.

"Who's screaming then?" The woman, who now were standing in the rooms doorframe, asked softly.

"Theo!" Madeleine giggled. The woman swiftly ran away.

"I don't like Theo, mommy just cares about him!" Madeleine complained. I nodded.

"I don't like him either!" I said and giggled.

I slowly sat up. Whats up with all these flashback dreams? I thought they were gone, but then they came back, after almost two years...

I went out of bed and started to search trough my bags for something to put on. A pair of black jeans and a matching tank top. Perfect.

My hair wasn't something I really wanted to deal with, so I made a messy bun with some help of a hair tie.

Let's go!

I went out into the corridor, with no idea of how I'll be able to find anything.

'TOAST!' Luceat shouted, and yes, somewhere someone were making toast. I followed the smell as my stomach was telling me to feed it.

When I was in a kitchen I saw Shaun standing at the toaster, making toast.

"Good morning!" He said and I answered with a 'morning'.

"You want toast?" He asked when the bread popped up from the machine.

"Hell yeah, Im starving!" He chuckled at my comment as he gave me one of the pieces.

"So, Stella..." He began.

"Oh no!" I groaned. He grinned evilly and asked me to give him the butter. Whoa, I am so scared!

"How old are you?" He asked as he smeared some butter on his toast.

"Fifteen." He nodded and put on a slice of cheese on his bread.

"How old are you?" I asked him and took a bite out of my toast.

"Seventeen." I nodded.

"Whats your real hair color?" He asked towards my hair.

"Brown-ish." I said and finished the toast. Shaun finished his too.

"What did your parents think when you dyed it?" He asked. I shrugged.

"What do you mean by that?" He asked, so many questions! Ugh!

"I've never met my parents, I got left in the forest as a baby." I said and shrugged once again.

"Oh..." He said as if he though I got sad.

"Its okey, Fate didn't want me to live with them... Or something." I said and chuckled. He smiled with his - oh so perfect - teeth.

"Hey, let's go meet my friends!" Shaun said, not letting me respond before he dragged me with him.

We went through lots of corridors before coming out from the house. On the grass, a few meters from the forest, a few teenagers stood. I assume they are Shaun's friends.

"Hey man!" A boy, around Shaun's age, with light brown hair said. All the teenagers looked to be the same age as Shaun. But after all, they were his friends - and probably classmates too.

"Who's she?" Another guy siad. He was really tall and had blond hair, like Shaun.

"This is Stella." Shaun introduced me to his group of friends.

"What's she doing here?" The brown haired guy said, kind of rude-ly.

"Uhm, I found her in the forest and I guess she's going to stay here for a while." Shaun said and the guy looked at me.

"Why were you in the forest?" He asked.

"Got banned from my pack." I said and shrugged. His eyebrows crashed together, questioning why.

"I rejected the alphas son as my mate." I explained and a girl, who I hadn't noticed standing there, smiled at me.

"I like her!" She said and I smiled back at her. "I'm Ivy" She said and I nodded. Her red hair was really pretty. Probably colored, like mine.

"And these two are Jupiter and Zane." As she spoke she pointed first at the brown haired boy and then at the tall one.

"We're going to go running. Wolf form." Ivy said.

"Hm..." I started.

"What?" She asked, as if something was wrong.

"I've never really showed anybody my wolf..." I said and their eyes widened.

"For how long..?" Ivy began, but didn't finish.

"Eight years..." I said lowly.

"But you're only fifteen, you couldn't have shifted at seven?" Everybody stood shocked.

"But I did." I said and shrugged. Everybody was quiet for a little bit.

"Well, sometime's gotta be your first to show it!" Ivy said and I bit my lip. Did I really want them to see it?

"I don't know..." I said nervously. "Only if we shift a bit into the forest." They all nodded and we started walking.

"Which color does it have?" Ivy asked. I gave her a smirk. "You'll have to guess."

"Grey?" I shook my head.

"Brown? White? Black? Caramel? Multicolored?" She kept asking me lots of different colors, but I just simply shook my head or said "no" until she gave up.

"Here!" Jupiter said and we stopped. "You first." He said and I nodded shyly. After I found a nice tree I went behind it and took off my clothes.

"I wonder how she looks!" Ivy said excitedly.

I felt my bones cracking and fur growing out on me. When I was on my paws I picked up my clothes and went out from the tree.

They all stood shocked in front of me.

"Wow!" Ivy said and walked up to me to feel my fur. Thats when I realized how big I was; I was almost as tall as her, and she wasn't short.

"Blue?" Zane asked, still as shocked as before. "B-but how? Thats impossible!" He looked like he had a headache.

"WHAT THE HECK!" Ivy screamed and took a step back.

"What?" The three boys said at the same time.

"T-t-the ey-eyes are r-reflections of t-the s-sky!"

... That explains a lot. I wasn't the only crazy person here! Yay!

I went behind the tree again and changed back into human, but something was weird. I had clothes on.

Suddenly everything became white. Was this how I was going to end?

"Greetings, Princeps Stellarum." A voice as smotheas honey said. My vision was blurry, but I could almost see a very beautiful woman in front of me.

"What?" I asked with a broken voice. I tried looking around, but everything was blurry and shining white.

"Who are you?" I asked her, she gave me a sad smile.

"We will meet again, Princeps Stellarum. But its time for you to leave." She said and bent down to give my forehead a soft kiss.

"Stella?" Someone screamed in my ear and slapped me.

"What the fuck." I said lowly as I opened my eyes. On me I had a white dress. It was very beautiful and had loads of silver colored and white colored gems on it.

"What the hell happened there?" Shaun asked me. I could tell he was really worried. "There was a big ass light beam and you were in the middle of it and then your body just dropped!" He said.

"And whats up with the princess outfit?" Ivy asked. "Its pretty though..." She said, looking at the dress in envy.

"I don't know..." I said an sat up.

What did that woman even say? "Princeps Stellarum"

Chapter 20

Shaun's POV

Stella went behind a tree, to change into her wolf. Apparently she has never shown it to anybody before.

All the way in to the forest, Ivy had tried guessing what color it is. Unfortunately Stella just shook her head and said "no" to every color Ivy asked.

When I heard someone breathe in quickly I looked up. My eyes met a wolf. It shocked me, not just the size, the color.

The wolf was blue goddammit! And it was the size of an alpha, but thats impossible. Stella was not an alpha. - Maybe thats why she never showed it to anybody, because it was so rare not even the oldest books have told us about them. I've heard so many stories and legends, but none has told me about a blue one.

"Blue?" Zane said, he was as shocked as everybody else. "B-but how? Thats impossible!"

Ivy stood next to Stella and petted her. They were almost as tall, and Ivy was just a little bit shorter then me.

"WHAT THE HECK!" Ivy suddenly screamed and took a step back from the magnificent wolf.

"What?" Me, Jupiter and Zane said at the same time. Did she hurt Ivy?

"T-t-the ey-eyes are r-reflections of t-the s-sky!" She stuttered and we all looked into the wolfs eyes. And Ivy wasn't lying, not at all. The eyes didn't even have a pupil, they just reflected the sky.

Stella went behind the tree again, to change back. But after a little while she wasn't back.

"Ste-" Ivy started, but didn't finish when a super big light beam showed up. In the light beam Stella's body, in a really sparkly dress, were floating upwards. When she was in the middle of it, maybe seven meters up in the air, she dropped down to the ground. But she didn't die, no bones cracked and she didn't get any wounds, by the looks of it.

"What the fuck..." Stella murmured when I had slapped her awake.

"What the heck happened there?" I asked her. Even though I don't know her at all, I should be worried. I mean; who drops from several meters and is completely ok?

"And whats up with the princess outfit?" Ivy added. "Its pretty though..." She was staring enviously at the dress.

I looked at the dress Stella had on. It was white with lots of crystals and gems on it, they were all white too. On her head was a silver colored tiara, with a little gemstone in it. If I'd say that she wasn't beautiful, I would be lying.

"I don't know..." She said and sat up, looking like she was thinking about something.

Suddenly, her eyes changed color to the same white as her dress. "Take me to your alpha." A woman's voice demanded. It wasn't Stella who spoke. Stella - no, this woman in her body - stood up and stared out in the forest in front of her. The eyes of her wasn't deep brown anymore, the iris and the pupil was gone. Replacing them was the color white, and it was shining.

"O-okay." I stuttered and started walking out from the forest, with the woman and my friends following me.

We were not that far away from the pack house, I could see it from behind the bushes and branches in front of me.

We walked up to the door of the pack house. 'Alpha, you need to come to the door!' I mind-linked him, to make him come here.

'Why?' He asked when he heard my frightened voice echoing in his head.

'NOW!' I told him, and shortly after that the door opened and he came out.

"T-this i-is our alp-pha." Jupiter said and we all looked towards our confused alpha.

"Wha- Uhm..." He noticed the woman, or Stella. "Excuse me?" He asked her. She bowed her head in respect.

"Alpha Winston." The woman's voice was really powerful, but not like an alphas or lunas. Powerful in another way.

"Hi?" Our alpha said, questioning who this was. He wasn't afraid at all, just confused.

'Doesn't he know who she is?' Max, my wolf asked. What did he mean by that?

"Take care of the princess." The woman said and then the glow from her eyes disappeared. Stella's body fell down at his feet.

"Wha-at?" Ivy said and crouched down to look if Stella was okay. Her hand slowly made its way up to her hair, to take all the hair out of her face.

Suddenly, Ivy screamed in pain and quickly retreated her hand. "The tiara is made of fucking silver!" She said as she hugged her hand. But why wasn't her head bruised and why wasn't she screaming in pain?

'She is unconscious, stupid!' I could see Max rolling his eyes at his own statement.

"We should get her to the pack doctor." I said and lifted her up in my arms. She still wasn't moving, but breathing. Everyone nodded as I started making my way to the little pack hospital which was located a few meter to the right of the pack house.

'Mel, I am coming to the pack hospital in a few secs with an unconscious girl.' I mind-linked Melody, our pack doctor. She responded with a 'ok' as I entered the little building.

"In here!" Mel said as she walked into a room. I followed her in and laid Stella down on the little bed in the right corner of the room.

"Wow." Mel said when she saw Stella. Probably shocked by the beautiful outfit of hers.

"Don't touch the tiara, its made out of silver." I said and gave her a meaningful look. "Ivy hurt her hand on it." I said and she nodded.

"She got possessed by a lady... And the lady said something like; Take care of the princess, to Alpha." I sat down on a chair in the other corner of the room. Stella has a lot to tell us when she wakes up.

"Hm, okey." Mel nodded and walked to a little cabinet by the bed. She was probably gonna give Stella some kind of medicines.

I looked at Stella. The long blue hair wasn't in the bun she had it in when she came to the kitchen this morning, it was all over the place. Her skin was a bit paler, making her look a bit more human-like. Her eyes were closed, so was the pink lips of hers. But suddenly they formed an 'o' and she groaned in pain.

"Shh." Mel hushed calmly. Stella's eyes flew wide open and she looked around. When her eyes met mine, she calmed a bit seeing a familiar person.

"Wh-what happened?" She asked and slowly sat up. Her hand flew up to her head as if she had a headache. "And what is this?" She said, pulling out the tiara from her hair. My eyes widened, how could she touch that?

"Stella? That thing is made out of silver." I said and she let go of it. When the tiara touched the floor a little cling noise filled the room.

"H-how didn't that hurt?" Her eyes widened and I could hear her heart start to beat faster.

"Shaun... Touch that." She said, pointing towards the little tiara on the floor. I bit my lip and went to pick it up, but dropped it as soon as I touched it. Pain, pain through my whole arm. A cry slipped out from my lips.

"Stella, is your wolf gone?"

Chapter 21

S tella's POV

"Stella, is your wolf gone?" Shaun asked me. My eyes widened, that could not be true. Just because silver didn't hurt me my wolf wasn't gone, right? As I started to think about a life without my wolf my heart started beating faster and I started to hyperventilate.

'Rude!' Luceat growled at Shaun. So she wasn't gone?

'Nope!' Luceat chuckled. 'You're not getting rid of me that easily!' Her chuckle turned into an evil laughter.

My breathing was normal by the time Luceat spoke. I tilted up my head from the floor to meet Shaun's eyes. Confidently I shook my head and showed him my wolf's eyes. When he saw them he nodded slowly.

"But why can you touch the tiara then?" He asked in confusion. I shrugged, I had no idea. Both of us stared at it in confusion.

'A princess who can't touch her tiara isn't a princess. Thats why you can touch your tiara. Because it's yours.' Luceat explained. What? But I am not a princess?

'Yes, yes you are.' Luceat was as serious as she could be. She must be speaking the truth.

"Because it's mine..." I said and picked it up. "The tiara is mine." I said and put it on my head, where it was on my head before I threw it away.

"What?" Shaun was really confused. He looked like he saw a llama give birth to a hippo through its mouth.

"I am a princess..." I whispered, now confused myself. How could I, a teenage werewolf girl, be a princess?

"What?" Shaun seemed to be talking with his wolf for a bit, before he bowed. The pack doctor did the same. I was really weirded out right now.

"We need to tell the alpha." Shaun said, dragging me with him out of the building. Before I could say anything we were in the pack house, walking to the alpha's office. Everyone we walked past bowed. It made me feel weird... It made me feel... Powerful.

Shaun stopped and knocked on a door, making a voice tell us to enter. When we were standing in the room I looked around. It was some kid of living room. In a coach some people, and the alpha, sat. They however didn't bow like the other people we had walked past in the house. It made Luceat mad, and she growled.

"Alpha." Shaun said and bowed to show his respect for his alpha. The alpha sat with his arm around a lady's shoulders. She was probably the luna of this pack.

"Shaun?" The alpha said, making it sound like a question. And it obviously was one too, he was asking why Shaun was here.

"And?" The alpha looked over at me, he had forgotten my name.

"Stella." Shaun filled in. "Princess Stella." He said. Everybody in the couch looked over at me.

"Princess?" The alpha asked. I nodded as an answer. He frowned. Luceat growled and the sound echoed in my head.

'Why are you growling?' I asked her, she didn't really growl that often compared to others wolfs. Luceat was more of the quiet type.

'Why are they not bowing? You're a princess!' She growled angrily.

'Chill. Its not like we can force them to bow in front of us!' I said, in hope of her calming down. But she didn't, she just chuckled evilly. After that the alpha and the others bowed, but it didn't look like they did it willingly.

"What the heck?" A red haired teenage girl whispered. "H-how did y-you?"

Luceat was laughing evilly, did she really force them to do that?

'No, their wolves did!' Luceat answered my thoughts. 'They don't want to disrespect you, but their humans wouldn't bow; so they forced them!' Luceat cleared up my confusion. For me.

"It wasn't me. It was your wolves." I said as I went to stand by the wall. Everyone in the coach looked like they talked to their wolves, so I didn't interrupt.

The alpha coughed after a few minutes, bringing everybody back from their thoughts. "So, princess." The alpha said, a little bit too rude for Luceat's liking. But I just nodded at him, letting him know he could say what he had to say.

"We have come to an agreement, you have permission to stay here for how long as you want. You can also join our pack whenever." The alpha then bowed.

After that I dragged Shaun out in the hallway. "Ok, so first of all. I. Hate. Dresses. Second, you know how to locate in this house." I said, and he knew what I was talking about, so he lead me to my room.

"Thanks Shaun." I said and gave him a smile, he smiled back. "I'll be nearby." He said and left.

As I got in to the room I heard someone gasp, it sounded like it came from the empty wardrobe in the corner of my room. Why would anyone be in there..?

Slowly I opened the door, revealing a little kid. Oh god, no. Not children.

"What are you doing here?" I asked, trying to sound nice. The kid, who was a little boy, laughed. He was kinda cute, like 'kid-cute'.

"I am hiding from my brother." He whispered. "Why do you have a princess dress? And a crown?" The little boy said.

"I am wondering that too, little boy. But please, can you get out of my closet. And my room too. I need to change, these clothes are horrible." By the 'my-clothes-are-horrible' part, I had lifted him up on my hip. Fortunately, he was just about 4 or 5 years old, and didn't weigh anything.

"Im Cabe, whats your name?" He asked as I put him down o the floor outside of my room. I gave him a little smile. "Stella." I answered him. "Bye Stella!" He said and then I closed the door. He was nice, and wasn't all weird and disgusting as other kids. Luceat nodded at my thought. She liked children who was nice.

Quickly I got out of the dress and put on a pair of grey sweatpants and a big dark red hoodie. My hair I pulled up in a bun, as I did this morning.

When I got out in the corridor I saw a couple of people there. Unfortunately I wasn't really a social butterfly, in my opinion. But I had to ask for directions.

I approached a woman who were walking down the corridor. "Excuse me, do you know the way... Uhm, somewhere really? I just moved in and I can't find anything." The woman smiled at me and I smiled back, to be nice.

"Of course. Im Welma." She said and started walking with my hand in hers, pulling me with her to wherever we were going. "Im Stella." I introduced myself and she nodded.

Welma was very good looking. She had a curvy body and really long, pretty, brown hair going down underneath her boobs. She wasn't dressed slutty or anything, she was dressed in some kind of clothes from a, what it looked like, expensive brand. Maybe she was some kind of fashonista?

"Here's the living room." She said and dragged me to the coach, where some people sat. Two guys and a girl. "This is Isaac, my mate." She said and pointed towards a big guy. "And this is Caleb." She said and pointed towards an even bigger guy. He had brown hair and grey eyes.

"And this is Livia, my best friend!" She said and pointed towards a little girl, probably the same height as me. Welma and her mate looked like they were around 20 and Livia and Caleb looked about 17. Why is everyone older than me here? Is there no one my age living in this pack house?

"And you are?" Caleb said rudely. I just smirked at him. "Stella." I said and put my hands in the hoodies pockets.

"Hey, are you not that girl who-" Isaac started, but I cut him off. "Has a weird colored wolf and was brought up in a light beam, several meters up in the air and fell down only to wake up in a princess outfit - yes." I said and their eyes widened.

"Has a weird colored wolf?" Livia asked shyly. I nodded, "I can show you it sometime, if you want to." I said and they nodded.

"Now! Pleas, please, please, pleas-" Livia and Welma started.

"Err, sure..." I said as they both dragged me out of the house with the boys trailing behind us. "But then you'll have to shift too, I want to go for a run." I said when we were outside.

The fresh air felt nice inside of my lungs. As we walked towards the forest I got to know a little bit about them all.

Caleb was the alphas son and Isaac was going to be his beta. Livia's mom was half human half wolf, Welma was actually a rouge before meeting Isaac.

"Lets shift here!" Caleb said and we all went behind trees and took off out clothes. The familiar sound of cracking bones went through my ears when I shifted. My clothes went into my mouth ad I walked out from behind the tree.

In front of me stood four wolves.

One big and beige with green eyes, Caleb.

One brown, little smaller, with brown eyes, Livia.

A kid of big one with light grey fur and blue eyes, Welma.

One a tiny bit smaller than Caleb's wolf. It had multicolored fur. Mostly grey, black and brown colors. The eyes were dark blue, Isaac.

They were all shocked when they saw my blue wolf. Caleb even dropped his clothes when he saw how big I was.

'We're bigger than him!' I could almost see the evil grin on Luceat's face. Although we were bigger than him, we were not that much bigger. Just about 10 cm.

To stop them from staring at me, I started running. Surprisingly, I was quicker than them. Only Caleb could run next to me. The other ones were running a few meters behind us.

He looked at me, as if he was challenging me. He started to run faster. I could tell that he was pushing himself to run the fastest he could. But I'm just jogging.

I let him think that he was faster than me for about a minute. Then I just sped up, running a few meters in front of him.

When nobody was running near me, I looked back. They wee staring at me. And at something else. That something else, guess what. I bumped into it.

But the weird thing was, it wasn't a thing. It was a wolf. Probably a rouge. He looked at me, shocked. After having him stare at me for a couple of minutes he got behind a big rock and changed.

"Shift." He demanded me, I went behind a tree and did so. I put on my clothes and went out to see what he wanted. There stood all my 'friends'. (Welma, Livia, Isaac and Caleb.)

"What do you want?" I asked the guy who stood in front of me in only a pair of basketball shorts. He didn't really smell rouge.

"Who are you?" He asked me. I looked up at his face. Why does everyone need to be so tall? He wasn't my age after all, but he was taller than me. He looked to be about 19 years old.

"Why are you wondering that?" I asked him. He smirked at me and put one if his hands on my right shoulder. "Because you're on my territory." He said.

"And?" I asked. His hand tensed.

"I am the soon to be alpha for the Unwanted's." He said. The unwanted's? I haven't heard of that before.

"We are a pack who lets anybody who feels unwanted join us." He explained.

"Oh..." I said, I was kind off one of those people. One of those who was unwanted.

"And who are you?" He asked.

"My name is Stella. I don't really have a pack at the moment. I got kicked out of mine last week." I said and returned him a smirk.

"And why did you get kicked out from it?" He asked. Apparently he was one of the curious ones.

"Err, nothing," I said sarcasticly. "I just rejected the soon-to-be Alpha as my mate." I said calmly. He frowned, probably thinking something like "Why would she do that?".

"You're free to join my pack, if you want to." He said and I smiled at him.

This will be hard...

Should I stay at the Shadow Wood pack?

Or should I go back to the Blood Moon pack, to all my nearest friends?

Or should I go and join the Unwanted's?

Chapter 22

I went behind a tree and changed back into my wolf, to run back. When the others saw that, they started running knowing I easily could catch up. And so I did.

When I was next to Livia, who was running a little bit slower than the others, I looked at her. She looks like she is thinking about something, even though she is in her wolf form.

'I wonder what she is thinking about...' Luceat said as she started thinking. I couldn't hear what she thought of, but I wasn't that interested really. All I was interested about right now was that pack.

Did they really let in anyone? Even really evil people? Even humans? No, no they can't let in humans in their pack. Except for the ones with werewolf mates. Otherwise, humans shouldn't know about us werewolf. Only if they are hunters.

"Are you going to shift back or not?" Caleb asked me. Apparently we were back at the pack house and everybody was in their human forms again. Slowly I nodded. Or at least tried to, it was quite hard to nod as a wolf.

Quickly I went behind a tree and changed.

"It's dinner right now." Caleb. said. I smiled. After that run, I was really hungry. My stomach craves food! But how did he know that it was dinner right now? My eyebrows crashed together, but he understood what I wondered, as if he read my mind. "My dad mind-linked me." He explained. I nodded and we all walked in to the house.

It smelled like hamburgers, something I haven't eaten in a long time. The last time I remember eating hamburgers was maybe three months ago. When I was at the Blood Moon pack. My friend Samuel and I went to some kind of fast food restaurant and ate because they wouldn't give us any food at home. They said something like, "If you throw eggs at everybody's houses at halloween, you don't get any food for a week!". We didn't really think that what we did was bad... I mean, it was just a prank. P, R, A, N, K. Unfortunately, they didn't think so. We ended up going to restaurants the whole week.

"Stella!" Shaun's voice woke me up from my thoughts as I walked into the kitchen. When I looked at him I gave him a friendly smile. "I see that you've met Caleb." He said and looked towards Caleb who stood on my left.

"Yep." I answered and sat down next to him. "His wolf is suuuper slow." I said making some people choke on their food. Shaun hit my arm. "He is the fastest running wolf in our pack." He whispered in my ear, making me laugh. "I am serious, Stella." Shaun said and I stopped laughing.

"I am super fast not super slow!" Caleb said from the other side of the table. I just smirked at him. "But I'm faster." I said.

"But your wolf is weird!" Caleb said, because he apparently was really bad at comebacks.

"No, she is beautiful and faster than yours." I said and heard someone chuckle.

"But my wolf is more powerful!" Caleb said. Well yeah, he is going to be a alpha.

'No, we are not less powerful than him.' Luceat chuckled. Maybe she can make him bow for me? He would freak out!

'Sure!' Luceat said evilly.

I smirked at Caleb as he bowed his head for me. Luceat's laugh echoed in my head when Caleb's expression looked like he had seen a ghost.

"Wh-what the hell?!" He said and I laughed. "ARE YOU A WITCH?!? YOU MUST BE!!!" He shouted. I shook my head. I wasn't a witch, but it would be awesome to be one though.

"No, no I am not a witch." I cleared out as everybody in the room was currently listening to our conversation. Caleb looked at Shaun, who was laughing.

I leaned over the table. "After the dinner I can show you." I said.

Shaun was still laughing at Caleb's confused face. "Stop!" Caleb said and kicked his leg making Shaun growl. Shaun looked at me and I rolled my eyes.

"Are they always like that?" I asked a girl sitting a few meters away. She nodded shyly and blushed. Uhh? Okey...

"Then I wont be staying here for long!"

"Why not?" A little voice said behind my back. I turned around to face whoever was standing behind me. It was the little boy who was in my closet before.

I shrugged as an answer and he looked sad. Why was he sad? Children are the only thing weirder than humans.

"Cabe what are you doing here?" Caleb groaned. The little boy looked up at Caleb. They looked very similar, probably siblings.

"I want to eat dinner too!" The little boy, Cabe I think his name was, said. Caleb groaned. "But then you can go to your friends, or mum and dad!" Caleb said. He obviously didn't like his little brother.

Cabe looked sad but muttered a "fine" to his big brother and ran away to some other kids.

"Is he your brother?" I asked Caleb, even though it was pretty obvious. Caleb nodded.

"I have another brother too, he's fifteen." Caleb said and turned towards another table to look at a guy who had similar hair and eyes to Caleb.

"So there is people my age here!" I said as I looked at the boys and girls sitting around the boy. Shaun chuckled at my comment.

"Zachary!" Caleb shouted, bringing the guys attention to him. "I've said it so many times; Don't call me that!" The guy said angrily. "But thats your name!" Caleb said making the guy even angrier.

"Anyways, Stella this is Zach. Zach this is Stella." Caleb said. Zach looked at me and smiled. I however didn't smile back.

"Hi, are you new here?" Zach asked. I nodded. "Mhm, I've been here for about a day or something." His smile widened. Oh god, he is probably the biggest fuck boy in the world.

"So you probably don't know how to find anything around here then?" Zach said, still smiling.

"I know the way to my room, the kitchen and out. Thats all I need to know where to go." I said, making him smile a bit less. He sat down next to Caleb, in front of me.

"You sure?" He said and winked. Winked? What is he doing? Is he sick?

"Yeah I am pretty sure." I said and leaned my head against Shaun's arm.

"You can always come to me if you need anything." He winked again. A load growl escaped my throat, making him jump back.

"Sorry, me and my wolf are allergic to fuck boys." I said. He glared at me before retreating to his laughing friends. Caleb and Shaun was laughing too.

"So your pack is full of fuck boys, nice." I said lowly, but of course Shaun heard and started to laugh harder. I glared at him and punched him in the stomach. He screamed. "Ouch! Why did you do that?" Me and Caleb just smiled at each other.

"So, do you want to see that thing?" I asked him and he nodded.

Slowly we walked around in the corridor. An awkward silence surrounded us, nobody had anything to speak of. I let my fingertips slightly touch the wall as we walked. Whenever a door interrupted the wall my fingers flew off it, and then back on when the door was behind us. Caleb was thinking about something, you could see it in his expression. He looked at my hand, but he clearly wasn't thinking about what I did with it. The most likely thing he could think off is probably what I am going to show him. I wouldn't be as calm as him if I was him. I mean, he doesn't know me. [OBJ]"Here's my room." I said as my hand grabbed the could handle and opened the door. Caleb looked around in the little room. It was just a bed and a closet with a bathroom connecting to it and the room next door.

"So what did you want to show me?" He asked curiously and looked me in the face. I smirked and then turned towards the closet. "A really weird thing."

Chapter 23

"A weird thing?" He asked, quoting what I just said. A nod was what I answered him with. I just wanted him to see it. My hands began to shake a tiny bit when they reached for the closet handle. Slowly I opened the closet door, revealing the dress. After I took it off I hung it in the closet, just so I wouldn't have to look at it. The tiara I left on a shelf over where the dress was hanging.

"Why do you have-?" Caleb asked, but I cut him off. I didn't really want to answer all off his questions. "Try to pick up the tiara." I demanded him. He frowned.

"Try to pick it up?" He asked, but did as I said when I glared at him. "Ouch! Thats silver!" He said, holding his hand just as Shaun did before today. And apparently Ivy too.

Easily I picked up the tiara. Caleb gave me some looks and murmured things like "how? but thats silver!".

"Its my tiara..." I said and put it on my head. "Apparently, I am a princess." I shrugged.

"A princess, what? Was that why my wolf demanded me to bow for you?" Caleb was confused. His eyebrows were tied together. I gave him a little smile.

"But please, don't tell anyone about it." I said and took off the tiara. He nodded as I put the tiara on the shelf and closed the closet. "You have my word on it." He said and held a hand on his heart. Not literally on his heart, on his chest above his heart.

"Good."

We walked out of the room and closed the door. "So where are we going now?" I asked him. He obviously knows the way around the house, so I could just follow him around for the evening.

"The pack usually goes for a run about now." He said and I nodded. Even though I've been out for a run earlier it could be nice to go for another.

"Shall we go out and join them?" He asked and I nodded. We started making our way out. I already knew how to get out. It was something I felt was important to know as soon as I get to a place.

After a couple of minutes we were outside of the house. There stood about a hundred people. They were probably the ones who was going on a run. As we walked into the crowd people bowed for Caleb. Not for me though, I didn't really want them to anyways.

"Caleb!" A high pitched voice screamed, making me jump back a bit. A girl, probably Caleb's age, who looked a bit slutty came up to him. "Hi, Caleb!" She said in the same tone. Her voice annoyed me, I am quite surprised that my ears aren't bleeding right now.

"Hi Vanessa." Caleb said. He didn't seem very excited. So this was one of the pack sluts? Caleb looked at me and confirmed that with a single raising of one eyebrow. Then he looked back at the girl, Vanessa I think her name was.

"Who's she?" She said rudely, towards me. Luceat growled and muttered something like, "don't disrespect a princess".

"This is Stella." Caleb said and turned towards me. Vanessa glared at me. She obviously wanted to have Caleb's attention.

"Okey..." She said. "Can I talk to her for a minute?" She said and winked at Caleb. He nodded, relieved that she was gone. For now.

"Okay, little girl. Keep your paws of my Caleb!" Vanessa said angrily. If they were mates, Caleb would've greeted her with a kiss and he wouldn't have been so annoyed around her. So he is not hers.

"Your Caleb? You two don't really look like mates to me." I said, if she could be rude. I could be too.

"You are a bitch!" She said. I wonder where she got that from, because last time I checked I was a virgin. 100% virgin then, 100% virgin now.

"I shouldn't disrespect me if I was you." I said, warning her. What would happen if she disrespected me? I don't really know. But when a pack member disrespects their alpha, thats no good.

"And why should I respect you? I bet your wolf is super weak and small." Vanessa said. I just chuckled at her comment. Caleb, who probably were overhearing our conversation chuckled too.

"Why are you laughing?" Vanessa asked Caleb, making him laugh even harder.

"Her wolf is bigger than mine, faster than mine and it wouldn't surprise me if it was stronger too!" Caleb laughed.

Vanessa's jaw dropped, the people who were overhearing conversations jaws dropped too.

"Show us then, show us your wolf." She said, trying to sound cocky. I nodded and went behind a tree. The clothes I had on, I took off. When I was naked I shifted. Luceat howled in happiness, she loved being out. I picked up the clothes in my mouth and went out to show myself to the people.

If I said that they were shocked before, when Caleb said how big and fast my wolf was, that was an understatement. Their mouths were open and eyes really widened. Caleb just smiled. And Vanessa, her expression was priceless. Her eyes were as big as oranges and her jaw was almost touching her boobs. Although her boobs were pressed up to almost her chin.

"Blue?" Some people murmured. Others were talking about how big I was.

I walked to Caleb, telling him to change with a look. Vanessa was still staring at me. She was speechless.

I heard many people gasp when Caleb came to stand next to me in his wolf form. I was clearly a little bit bigger than him. Then people started to go behind trees, changing into their wolves. I assume that Caleb had said something through the mind-link.

Vanessa's wolf was much smaller than mine. Her wolf was white, too bad I've never liked white wolves. The eyes was blue. And to my liking, she was very slow and couldn't keep up with Caleb even when he jogged.

I ran around looking at the other peoples wolves. Many of them were grey. Thats a color I love on wolves, it's such a basic color but still so pretty. I counted the brown ones, I got to 11. The grey ones I didn't even bother to count, they were easily over 40. The rest 40 wolves was other colors. Some blond, caramel, multicolored, white and two black.

Swiftly I ran between lots of wolves. The wind stroke my fur and Luceat howled in enjoyment. And so I did.

I looked around, in a bush a few meters away a wolf was standing. It looked at us while we ran. But I had stopped running. Slowly I was walking towards the wolf in the bush. When it noticed me it started to walk backwards, until it hit a tree. You could tell that it wasn't from Caleb's pack.

The wolf was black with a few white spots on its left ear. I sniffed the air, it didn't smell rogue.

I went behind another bush and shifted back, putting on my hoodie. The hoodie was almost down to my knees, so I didn't put on my leggings.

"Shift." I said to the wolf. And so it did. In front of me was a man, a very tall man. But I don't think that he is a man, yet. He must be around 17, like Caleb and Shaun.

"What were you doing in the bush?" I asked him, looking up at his face. He had a couple of scars on his face and chest. The rest of his body was covered up by the bush.

He shrugged, "Why do you want to know?".

"Because you were literally spying or staring at this pack." I said and he smirked.

"Your wolf is cool." He said. Why did he even say that?

"Err, okay. But why were you looking at this pack?" I said and placed my hands on my waist.

"My alpha wanted me to find a blue wolf, and tell it that it needs to come with me." He said.

"And why should I come with you?" I asked him. This was weird, his alpha told him to get me?

He shrugged and ran his hand through his black hair. "Just come with me and you can talk to him. He just told me to get you." He said. I nodded slowly.

"Okay... I guess I'll come then..."

Chapter 24

I put on my leggings, ready to go with this man-ish boy to meet his alpha. While my thoughts wondered all over the place he stared at me. Just stared at me...?

Caleb and other wolves had realized that this guy and I was talking and growled at him. Swiftly, I ran to Caleb and petted his head. "Shhh, Caleb he is not going to hurt anyone." I said, trying to calm him down. But only a mate could calm him down, and I was defiantly not his mate.

"I will be gone for a little while. Unfortunately, I don't know for how long." Removing my hand from Caleb's wolf I looked at the other wolves who had stopped. "You can go back running." I said and then turned back to Caleb. "Bye, for now." I turned around once again, but to fave this guy.

"Let's go then." He said and shifted into his wolf again. But I didn't shift into mine, I'm fairly sure that I can run next to him even in human form. Luceat insisted, 'We can!' she said and that was what got me confident in it. So I started to run after the black wolf.

We didn't run for long, we ran shorter than I thought we would run. I wasn't even sweaty at all. The guy shifted back and put on a pair of shorts before I could take a look at him. "This way." He said and started walking in the direction of a massive house, probably the pack house.

Inside there was a lot of people, from the age of a couple of months to elders. Everybody looked different, some people had scars and some looked like the friendliest things in the world. Some was laughing and others growling.

We were in a big room, I don't know what kind. There was no sign for it to be a kitchen nor somewhere to eat, there was no sign for it to be a living room nor a bed room. It was just a room filled off pack members.

The guy, who I was following, grabbed my wrist and dragged me a few meters before I started to walk by myself. He suddenly stopped, causing me to crash into him. My nose hurt when I pulled back. A hand of mine flew up to it, to reassure that it wasn't at all broken. A small sigh left me as I could feel that it was completely whole. It was just hurting from crashing in to this guys muscular arm.

"Alpha, the girl is here." The guy said. While I was assuring myself that my nose was okay, he apparently knocked on a door. In the room he had pulled me into was a desk and a bug chair with a guy in it, he was strangely familiar. But then it hit me, it was the guy from the forest. The guy who was telling her that she was on his territory and that he was the soon to be alpha, even thought he wasn't. This guy dragging me here just called him alpha, which means that he is the alpha for this pack.

I groaned, "Not you again." There was a chair in front of the desk, I took the opportunity and sat down. After so much running today I was a little bit tired.

The alpha chuckled. "You can leave us now, Charles." He said and the guy who dragged me here walked out and closed the door. When we couldn't hear his footsteps anymore the alpha spoke, "I heard that you didn't have a pack." He was holding a pen in his hand, focusing on it moving side to side between his fingers. I nodded.

"Would you like to join mine?" He stopped playing with the pen and laid it down on his desk. His face had a serious expression on it. As an answer, I shrugged. "What do you mean by that?" He asked.

"I don't know. I might want to go back to..."

"The Shadow Wood pack? I understand tha-" Before he could finish I cut him off, I didn't know if I wanted to go back to them or the Blood Moon pack.

"No, no I don't know. Either them or... Another pack." I said and he nodded. He put his hands behind his head and leaned back in the office chair.

"So..." He didn't know my name. I gave him a weak smile, "Stella." He nodded.

"So, Stella. Tell me; how is your wolf blue?"

"I don't know, not even my wolf does." I said shyly and shrugged. Luceat and I had tried to figure out this blue mystery for years now, with no clue.

"Okay, are you sure you don't want to join my pack?" He asked.

"I never said I didn't want to, I just said that I didn't know." He nodded slowly at my choice of words. Then he took the pen up between his fingers again and let it wiggle back and forth.

"You should join my pack. We don't torture rogues, we let them join our pack. Not like those... Others." I nodded. Right now I really didn't know what to do, but to nod.

He smiled, "So you are? You are joining us?" He said, he was really excited for some reason. Like a dog when it knows that it will get treats. But he's partly dog, but I am no treat. I am a girl.

"Let me reconsider it for a minute, my wolf needs to agree with my decisions." He understood me as he nodded.

'What do you think?'

'It feels safe here, in some way. I know for sure that he wont try to hurt us.' Luceat got me convinced of that. It was good that she felt the same as me, safe around here. I think I might stay here.

'I think so too, Stella.' Luceat said. I mentally smiled at her, she was one of my best friends. I guess you need to get to know someone when you're stuck with them in your head. Luceat growled, and I laughed.

"Okay, I will join your pack." I said slowly and his smile was almost as big as his face. Why was he so excited by me joining his pack? His pack and the Shadow Wood's probably betted on who could get me to join their pack first. Neighboring packs are usually like that.

"Let me show you to your new room." He stood up and walked to the door, I did so too.

We walked out into the corridor and walked for a few minutes. This place is like a maze, I wont be able to find anything in here. I am quite sure of that.

"Here it is." He said and opened a door, revealing a big room with a queen sized bed in the middle of it. A queen sized bed? Is he out of his mind? I am not worth that.

"But I need to go back and get my bags and my-"

"No, we will send a guard to do that for you." He said and pushed me in the room, forcing me to look around.

"There is one thing that he can't pick up, I need to get it myself." I said, trying to convince this man to let me go back and tell the others what was going on.

"And, tell me Stella, why wouldn't he be able to pick this thing up?" The alpha asked curiously, but still angrily.

"It is made out of silver." I said and he frowned, "Why would you go there to pick it up, when you can't either?" I didn't really want to tell this pack about the princess thing, and I wont either. They will be absolutely uninformed. If I get some very good friends here, I might tell them.

"I can pick it up." I said and growled lowly. Unfortunately, he had heard my growl and growled back - not as quiet as me though.

"Don't disrespect your alpha!" He said in his alpha tone. I just chuckled, making him confused. "Why are you laughing?" He asked, no, he demanded.

"Oh, alpha, you know nothing about me." I said and closed the door in his face. He let out a scary loud growl, and probably woke up many people too.

Slowly walking to the bed I could feel how exhausted I was. I could feel it in my legs, in my arms and in my head.

As I fell into the bed I could feel the sleepiness taking over. When I finally laid down comfortably in bed I fell asleep.

Chapter 25

"Today, class, we will introduce ourselves to each other. We will say our name, what our mum and dads names are, if you have siblings tell us their names too. Then we will say our favorite animal, food and color. Let's start with you!" The woman with round glasses and crazy hair pointed at the boy who was sitting to her left in the circle on the floor.

"My name is Jacob." He said, but it sounded more like he said Jeicab. "My mum she is Carol and my dad is Blake. I have a big brother, his name is Sven and he has a bike! It's super cool and sometimes he lets me go on it with him!" The little boy named Jacob said and giggled. The teacher smiled at him with her weird smile, she showed some teeth. The ones she had left, she only had about 15 teeth.

"My favorite color is green and my favorite food is pasta with bacon and I like bears. Bears are big and cool!" He said and when he mentioned that the bears were big he made gestures with his hands to show how big they were.

"Okay, thank you Jacob. Now it's you turn." The teacher pointed at me and I felt nervous.

"I am Stella. My parents... I have never met my parents." I said and looked down. Sad, the emotion sad was all over me.

"What?" A little girl asked, "But you got born out of your parents?" The little girl got me even sadder.

"Let Stella say the rest of her things before we other speak, okay?" The teacher asked the group, but the question was pointed towards the little girl. The girl nodded and everybody looked back at me.

"My favorite color is blue, my favorite food is tacos and my favorite animal is wolves." I finished. Ever since I could remember, I've felt a weird connection towards wolves.

"Wake up!" Someone jumped on me screaming. I quickly sat up and let out a scream, who the hell just jumped onto me screaming at me to wake up?

"Err, excuse me, but who are you?" I asked the boy laying on my feet. He chuckled and shook his head. He was my age, and he was kind of good looking, like everyone with werewolf traits.

"And why did you scream at me and jump on me?" He stood up and stared at me, as his face slowly turned red.

"S-sorry." He said and ran out of my room. Why did he do that?

"Alicia, I was going to wake you up but I went into the wrong room and woke someone else up. But, Alicia, that girl looks exactly like you! Besides her hair!" I couldn't help to overhear their conversation, but I just heard that boys voice. The girl I assumed maybe talked to lowly for me to hear.

"Yes! No, that wouldn't make sense. She will probably be at breakfast, we'll see her there and you will se how much you two look alike!"

The boy was talking really loudly, I bet any shifter around here could hear what he said.

I sighed, wondering what this day will be like. As I sat up I noticed that my bags were placed on the floor. The tiara and dress wasn't there. Today, I will have to talk to whoever got my stuff here and ask them about the wardrobe.

The clothes I had on was very comfy, but they were really dirty and I still didn't have underwear on.

I put on some new underwear and another hoodie, a navy blue one, and another pair of leggings. Most of my clothes was hoodies, leggings, t-shirts and jeans.

My hair was still really messy, so I put it up in yet another messy bun.

In the corridor I couldn't find anything. After a few minutes of me being confused and walking around, I could smell something very familiar. Bacon.

I followed the scent and began to think of yesterday, when I followed the smell of Shaun's toast. But this time I came to a big room, with lots of people in it. Everybody was talking and laughing in there. Nobody stopped with what they were doing when I came in, besides the alpha.

"Quiet, everybody!" The alpha said loudly in his alpha tone, and right after that the whole room was quiet. All you heard was people breathing.

"This," The alpha stood up and pointed his finger towards me, causing me to begin to panic a little bit. "Is Stella. She is a new member of this pack." The alpha said.

"And? Why are you introducing her? You never introduce new people to us!" A man, the alphas age, said. The alpha smirked at him.

"Because Stella here, has a special wolf." The alpha said. Right now I just wanted to turn around, because everyones eyes were at me, staring at every move I made.

"And what do you mean by 'special wolf'?" Another man asked. The alphas smirk was directed towards me now.

"Yeah, Stella, what do I mean by special?" The alpha said.

"C'mon. It is not special just because of its color!" I said and sighed.

"But what about the size then? And the speed of it?"

Everybody in the room was giving me curious looks. I shrugged, "I am just well fed, I guess?" It sounded more like a question than I would've wanted it to. The alpha shook his head, still with that same smirk on his lips.

'He is crazy, I don't like this. It felt better yesterday...' Luceat whimpered and she got me even more nervous.

"Shift." The alpha demanded in his alpha tone. Something inside of me felt disrespected?

I shook my head, "No." The alpha looked confused. "I am your alpha, you need to obey my orders!" He shouted, in his alpha tone.

"No." My voice sounded a bit weird. "No, I wont obey you." I said and glared at him. Many people around gasped for air.

The alphas face turned red, he was angry. "Now!" He screamed, still with his alpha tone. It had no effect on me what so ever.

"No." I said calmly, something inside of me made me feel peaceful. Luceat wasn't whining anymore, she was smirking. Or at least trying to, she is a wolf not a human after all.

The alpha ran forward with his hands closed together, he was going to punch me. And it was going to hurt. For him.

Chapter 26

He ran, really fast, to me. But when he was almost two meters in front of me, he ran in to something. The weird thing was; there was nothing there. He ran in to open air, but got knocked back and fell down on the floor. It wasn't me who groaned in pain, it was he. He didn't hit me, he hit himself. On something invisible.

Many people gasped, staring at their alpha who was laying on the floor. He quickly stood up and looked around at the crowd. His eyes wondered over every single person, until he came to look into a woman's eyes. She looked back at him, angrily. Why was she angry?

"Cylinda!" The alpha said angrily, but he was still not looking away from the woman's eyes. "Cylinda, why did you do that?" He asked her and started to walk to her, but not letting his eyes slip off hers.

"You can't just make the poor girl shift when she clearly doesn't want to!" The woman made gestures with her arms and hands as she spoke to the alpha who now was standing in front of her. Everybody in the room was staring at them, overhearing their conversation.

"I am your alpha, you shouldn't question my actions!" The alpha stated angrily. His eyes didn't show anger, no, they showed love.

"And I am your luna, and mate, and you shouldn't question my actions either! Jim, calm down. You are embarrassing yourself in front of your pack!" The last part she whispered. I shouldn't have heard that, werewolf or not, but I did. So the alpha is called Jim.

"Can you come over here, please?" She looked really friendly, the woman. And her name was cool, Cylinda. I've never heard that name before.

I nodded before I, slowly, made my way to the couple. Staying a little bit to the left, to avoid alpha Jim, I smiled at Cylinda. Everything about her was friendly. Her red curly hair, the pair of blue eyes she had and even the slightly croaky nose of hers. It was all friendly. But after all, she is a luna. The packs mother, with other words.

"So, tell me, why does Jim want everybody to see your wolf?" Cylinda asked with a friendly smile. Jim growled, making Cylinda glare at him before looking back at me again.

"Because it is-" Jim started. Cylinda cut him off, "I was talking to her!" She said and pointed at me. He nodded and looked down at the floor, I could hear a little whine come out of him, as if he was ashamed.

"It is... A pretty color." I said shyly and put my right arm on my left one, to squeeze it a little bit. My eyes suddenly felt very interested in what the floor looked like, did it have a nice color? Was it dirty?

I got scared when some kind of force made my head fly up to meet Cylinda's eyes. She gave me a small smile.

'Haven't you realized it yet?' Luceat said, she sounded really annoyed at me. I couldn't figure out what she was talking about, realized what?

'She,' Luceat began and made me look at Cylinda's face, 'Is a witch.' Luceat explained to me. Oh, so that was what her and Jim's weird conversation was about...

"What color?" She asked, not that curious at all. It seemed like she just wanted to eat her breakfast right now, her eyes were practically screaming 'I don't want to be here!'.

"An unusual one..." I said, trying to avoid the question. Cylinda bit her lip, knowing that it wont be easy to get the information out of me.

"What color?" This time she used her Luna-tone on me. Just as the Alpha-tone, it didn't work.

"An unusual one, I said!" I repeated. Her eyes widened, probably because her using her special tone didn't work.

"How? Don't every pack member have to do anything we say when we speak with our tones?" Cylinda asked Jim. He nodded slowly and then he looked at me and spoke, "It doesn't work on her though... It's like she doesn't even listen..."

I shrugged as an answer, I don't know either. It was just a big mystery as why my wolf is blue.

"Err, and by the way, whoever got my stuff here for me forgot something..." I said to Jim. He frowned and turned around to look at a guy. And guess what - he was really well built. He had black hair and green eyes.

"John? Why didn't you get all of her stuff?" Jim asked the guy, who was called John. John put his hands up in the air. "I got everything that was in there!" John said and I shook my head.

"What did he miss to take with him?" Cylinda asked. Our eyes flew to her and I looked down.

"He wouldn't have been able to pick it up anyways..." I mumbled and bit my lip.

"What do you mean?" The three asked. I smiled, for a second, down at my shoes.

"Silver." I explained and they nodded slowly, all three.

"What was it?" Jim asked me, probably because someone would have to pick it up and get it here later today.

"I would rather not tell anyone-"

"What was it?" Both Jim and John asked. John was curious, I could tell it. You could easily see it in his eyes too, plane curiousness. He would probably be the one who would be ordered to get it.

"Just... A thing... And a dress, but that is not made out of silver..." I said slowly.

"Okay, John will go and pick it up later toda-"

"Can I come with him?" I asked, I wouldn't like him to see the tiara and dress. He would ask a million questions about it, and I wouldn't want to answer any of them. Plus, I never had the time to say goodbye to my friends over there, they are probably super worried about what happened to me.

"No!" Jim said. "Yes!" John said, they spoke exactly at the same time which got me confused. Would I go there or not?

"No." Jim said, making both John and Cylinda glare at him. "Okay, okay then!" He groaned.

"Let's go right now!" John flew up from his seat and ran towards me, with a big smile on his lips. However, the smile didn't show his teeth. It was just a little smile, on his lips.

I smiled back at him and followed him through some corridors. He stopped at a door with a sign on it that said "Garage". That reminded me, my motorbike is still at their house, just sitting there.

"Oh, and we need to get my motorbike too. But it probably doesn't have any gas in it..." I said and John nodded as he opened the black door.

In the garage there was three cars, one sporty matte black car and two range rovers. Cars isn't anything that I'm interested in, and I don't know a lot about them either.

"We're going to take my car," John pointed at the white range rover. I nodded and studied the car in front of me. "That," Now pointing at the sports car, "Is the alphas car, and that," He said pointing at the other range rover, "Is the betas car." I nodded.

"And if you haven't figured it out yet, I am the third." He said and opened one of the doors for me. Quickly I got into the car and sat down. Fortunately, the seat belt was easy to put on.

Before John jumped into the car he pressed a little button on the wall, making the wall in front of the car slowly move upwards until the car would be able to go out.

"Let's go then." John said as he closed the car door and then put on his seat belt.

Chapter 27

The car ride was short, or at least shorter than I thought it would be. John was sighing and annoying himself at the traffic. It seemed like many people was driving on this rode at this time of the day, which annoyed him. For me it wasn't very horrible, I could sit here all day. Just the thought of coming back to the Shadow Wood's and saying, "Uh, yeah, I joined the Unwanted's while I was gone. I'll just get the stuff John missed and then leave!" That thought makes me nervous. What will they think of me when I've said that? The two pack obviously doesn't like each other that well. At least from what I've snapped up from the almost two days being here.

"So, Stella, can you tell me what that silver thing is?" John's question snapped me out of my thoughts. I looked up at him and shook my head, I will not tell him. Not now, and not for as long as... I don't want to tell him about it. He sighed loudly as he frowned at the road.

"Why not?" He asked me, still looking at the road. Sometimes he looked to the sides, to read the signs to see if we were going the right way. I bit my lip and looked out the window, "Maybe I don't want you to know why."

"And why is that?" He took a quick look at me, with a little smirk on his lips. My hands started to drum on my thighs, thinking of an answer for him. It was an easy question, and I could just answer with an answer just as easy. But I don't want his curiosity to grow, or even exist. I want it to disappear in to thin air, unfortunately that's not how it goes.

"Secret." I answered, it was a bad answer to his question. The curiosity only grew inside of him, he practically smelled curious. I groaned at his excitement, "Someone will probably tell you when we are there, accidentally."

He nodded slowly as he made a left turn. My eyes went to concentrate themselves on the trees swishing by outside of the car window. I counted the trees, one tree, two trees, three trees, four trees. My eyelids felt heavy, so I closed them. Slowly the darkness which was surrounding me turned into a field filled of flowers.

The brown haired girl in front of me was chasing a butterfly purple as lavender. She didn't look down at the ground for a second, she was very focused on this pretty creature flying in front of her. I followed the giggling girl, she had a yellow dress on her. Before I could study her looks more, she tripped over the dress and fell down in the grass. But the girl wasn't crying, she wasn't sobbing or screaming. The girl was laughing, and so did I.

"Stella, Stella!" She shouted at me to come to her. I ran the same way as she ran just a minute ago, however I didn't fall on my blue dress. The girl was still lying down on the grass, looking down at something. "Stella, look!" The girl showed me a flower. I gasped when I saw it, swiftly I laid down beside her on the grass. We were both staring at the beautiful flower in front of us.

The flower was as beautiful as the day, it was sparkling and shimmering. The flower looked almost like a rose, but much prettier. It was brown whit hints of white in it. Even though brown is quite an ugly color, this flower was not.

I looked to our left, there was another flower. Just as pretty. "Look!!" I said and pointed at the other flower. It wasn't far away, my tiny arm was almost as long as the gap between them. The other flower was just as beautiful. But it didn't remind me of the day, it reminded me of the night. This flower wasn't sparkly and shimmery. It was dull. The color was stunning though. Blue, dark blue. The flower had some tiny white and yellow spots on it. It was the same kind as the other flower. We had both never seen anything alike.

"I've never seen these kind of flowers before..." She said, I nodded in agreement. The stunning flowers was also very unique, they looked a bit like roses, but still nothing alike them at all. "They can be out flowers. We'll call them the Stella and Maddie flowers!" We both laughed.

"Yes! And they are just for us, the sparkly one is yours and the blue one is mine!" I said. She was clearly very attracted to the sparkly flower, she admired it like it was something she couldn't touch or it would break. I liked the other flower the best, it felt like we had some kind of connection.

"Stella, we're here now!" John said and woke me up. I nodded tiredly. These flashback dreams are very confusing, are they supposed to tell me anything? They were just old memory's, mostly those with Madeleine in them. Although Maddie is a person who I love more than anything, it is very weird. Doesn't werewolf who reject their mate have nightmares about them? Or is that just yet another fake rumor?

"Stella!" John shouted in my ear when I didn't answer him or react to him speaking. My head snapped towards him, "What?" I asked. He chuckled at me.

"We are here now." He said and pointed at the familiar house outside of the car. I looked at the mansion in front of me and sighed.

"Let's go inside and get your stuff that I missed." He said and I nodded, we'd have to go in eventually. He opened his door and went out, to wait for me to join him. I took off my seat belt and sighed again.

"Are you coming or not?" John asked me and then closed the door. I glared at him and opened my door. When I stepped out of the car I could smell rain. It had probably rained while we were driving. I don't mind it though, I love the smell of rain.

"Should we go in?" John asked from the other side of the car. I nodded, "Yeah." We walked into the house, the door wasn't even locked. Didn't they have safety rules or something here? My pack had. They were things like, "Don't leave doors unlocked." and "Don't go out for a run all by yourself."

I heard fast footsteps in another part of the corridor, coming our way. Even though I'm not scared of what is coming towards us, I took a step closer to John. He had also realized that something or someone was coming our way. His heartbeat sped up a little bit, not mine. He was clearly a little bit scared.

"Stella!" I heard people shout, and then I was on the floor. When I opened my eyes again I saw four familiar faces, Ivy, Shaun, Caleb and Cabe had jumped on me. They all hugged me, making me unable to move.

"We didn't think that you'd come back!" Ivy said, with a little sad tone in the bottom of her stomach. The boys nodded sadly and Cabe ran forward, to hug my leg.

"But I did!" I said and gave them a wide smile. They all smiled back at me.

"For how long will you stay?" Caleb asked. I wanted to give him an answer, but I didn't have one. John and I only planned to get my stuff, but now I almost want to stay a bit longer. After being here for only about a day, I had made some friends. What did I even think when I joined the Unwanted's?

Chapter 28

I looked at John, with a look asking for how long we will stay. Hoping that he would say something like a couple of hours. He shrugged, "We were just going to get those things that I missed."

"Alright..." I said and gave my friends a sad smile. They returned one each, and Caleb looked down at the floor.

"Uhh, so where's the room then? I've forgotten." John said and scratched his neck.

"This way..." I said lowly and started walking. Past the living room, past the kitchen, to the left ant then to the right.

"Here it is." I said and placed my hand on the cold handle, then pushed it down. The door creaked when I opened it. When I saw the room again I noticed that nobody had touched a thing, besides the bed which was made.

"So what did I forget to pick up?" John asked as he looked around in the room, not noticing anything that could belong to me.

"Just a couple of things..." I said as I opened the wardrobe. The dress was hanging there, and the tiara was not touched.

"Why do you have those things?" John asked from behind me, I had forgotten that he was there for a second. I turned around to face him, "I ask myself that question too."

"What do you mean by that? Is it something you regret buying?" He asked as he looked at the gemstones on the dress. I shook my head.

"It must have been really expensive..." He was standing beside me now, wanting to take a closer look at the dress. I could tell that he hadn't seen the tiara yet.

I shook my head again, making him frown. "How could it not have been expensive? It has gems all over it!" He looked at me, making me chuckle a little bit. He looked quite silly when he frowned.

"I didn't buy it." I told him. He nodded slowly, but he was still frowning.

"So someone bought it for you?" I shook my head once again. I really don't know where it's from.

"Did you steal it?!?" He took a step back, thinking that I was a thief. I shook my head and chuckled at his reaction. "But you said that it was yours?"

"Honestly, I don't know how I got it." I said and turned back to the wardrobe. The dress is yet another mystery in my life.

"And what is that?" John said, pointing at the tiara on the shelf over where the dress were hanging. So now he notices it.

"Just another of my things." I said and took the dress off of the hanger. He frowned, "Let me get it for you then..." I was just about to stop him, when he screamed. His hand touched the tiara right when I was going to speak.

"Ouch! Why do you have a silver thing?" John asked as he was shaking his hand. It smelled burnt flesh, even though he just touched the silver for a second.

"I said that I had a silver thing, right?" He nodded and looked back up at the tiara. His eyes wasn't focusing on it though, he was in his thoughts.

After a minute he snapped out from his thoughts and turned his head towards me, "But how will we get it out of here?" His head turned back and now he was looking at the tiara. "Why do you even have a tiara, in silver?" He asked. His grey eyes looked back at me, asking if I had any ideas.

"Hm, I don't know." I began, "But it will be easy getting it out of here." I said and reached up for the tiara and grabbed it. John's eyes widened.

"How?" He asked, I answered him with a simple shrug and left the room. John had to run to catch up with me, and he did. When he was walking besides me he looked at me, curiously.

"Hm, can you keep secrets?" I asked him. He frowned once again, but nodded.

"Maybe this will make you understand." I said and made him bow. When I let him control his body again, he looked terrified.

"Wait? Are you a werewolf-witch hybrid?" He asked and dragged a hand trough his dark hair.

I rolled my eyes and shook my head, "No, dumbass. Ask your wolf instead."

'He can ask his wolf, right?' I asked Luceat.

'Mhm.' She answered, she sounded like she was doing something else and didn't relly care about me.

'Well, I am actually doing something. Bye!' She said and disappeared. Well, I will probably don't see her for a while then.

"What?!?" John gasped, "You're a princess?!?" I nodded and turned around, to go to the car.

"We need to tell Alph-"

"No, no we don't." I said, he nodded as if I was his alpha and just used my alpha tone on him.

"Let's just go to the car."

The ride back was longer than I wanted it to be. It was filled with loads of questions from John, which I didn't know half of the answers to. Halfway trough the car ride, I didn't bother to answer his questions anymore.

I leaned my head against the window, and looked out. The sky, which usually was bright blue, is dark. The color of my wolf, but a little bit darker. I wonder if you could compare her eyes to the sky, but I still don't know the color of them.

The darkness revealed all of the thousand stars. They were now shining at us, and I tried to find some zodiac signs. I could find the one called Big dipper, but none of the others I could. The car was moving to fast and all the trees beside the road were covering the stars.

I decided to get some rest, and closed my eyes. Shortly, I could feel me getting more tired each second.

"Stella?" The little girl said. She was standing in front of me and leaning against a wall.

I looked up at her and nodded as I gave her a smile. She smiled back at me and came to sit down on the wooden bench I was sitting on. We both turned our bodies, so we looked into each others eyes.

"You know about the mind-link thing, right?" I nodded at her and she gave me a half hearted smile.

"And you know that it doesn't work for you?" I nodded once again, this time her smile was warming.

"But you and me, we can talk in our heads, right?" She asked. A big smile spread itself all over my lips, and I nodded again.

"That is mind-linking, the doctor said that you can do it with me, but nobody else. She also said that she don't know why you only can do it with me." The little girl said. We smiled at each other.

"It's okay. You're my best friend Maddie, and I like that only you can mind-link me!" I said it seriously, and the atmosphere felt serious. Until I giggled, and we both went happy.

"I wish you were my sister! Instead of Theo being my brother!" I agreed with a nod.

The car stopped, and woke me up. Swiftly I unlocked the seat belt and opened the car door. Then I covered the tiara with the dress, and went inside of the house.

While I was walking through the corridor, many people took a curious look at the shimmering piece of fabric and gems in my hands. I had folded it around the tiara, and you couldn't see that it was a dress.

"Stella!"

Chapter 29

I froze.

What does he want me? Couldn't we just ignore each other the whole day? No, Alpha Jim seems a bit obsessed with me. In some way.

"What?" I asked him, still walking. He sighed and I heard him walking towards me. I stiffed when his had was placed on my shoulder. My legs stopped moving and my heart skipped a beat or two.

"Ste- What is that?" He asked. He was clearly going to say something else, but when he saw the fabric in my arms he asked about it instead.

"Nothing." I said, fully recovered from the shock of him having his hand on my shoulder. I started walking again, but he followed. What did he want?

"What is it?" He attempted to get me to tell him what it is by using his alpha tone, and he miserably failed. My old alpha could use it on me and it worked, so why couldn't he? Honestly, I am kind of relieved that his tone doesn't work on me. He asks questions which I don't want to answer.

"What. Is. It?" He asked angrily. Unfortunately, for him, he isn't going to get to know what it is I am holding, because I ain't telling him.

He touched the fabric and tried to get it out of my hands, but my grip was too tight. But he didn't stop pulling the fabric towards him. The dress couldn't handle the pressure, it broke. There was now a big hole in the middle of it. Luceat was furiously growling and cursing.

'He destroyed our dress!' She sounded both angry and sad. I tried to calm her down by humming a lullaby for her, one that I knew she liked. Her breathing slowed down a bit and she stopped cursing and shouting.

Jim didn't look sad at all, he was still pulling the dress towards him. What if I went to throw the tiara at him? He would get really hurt by getting hit by it and by touching the silver!

I unfolded the dress and got the tiara out. Before he could react I let go off the dress and he flew to the floor. I threw the tiara at him. His scream filled the whole corridor as I ran up to him and pressed the tiara to his face. When he started crying in pain I retreated to my room, with the dress and the tiara.

I slammed the door shut and locked it with the key hanging on the wall beside it. It wont be long until I get banned from this pack too... But now it will be because of the alpha destroying my stuff.

"Stella!" I heard a woman shout from outside the door, and then I heard someone bang on the door. "Stella, please let me in!"

I didn't open the door, instead I packed down the dress and the tiara in one of my bags.

When I closed the bag I heard a weird noise from my door, and the second after it flew open. In the doorway Cylinda stood. Oh god, she is probably pissed off right now.

"Can you show me that dress?" She asked and then received a quiet "no" from me.

"Stella, I promise that I wont destroy it." She said, and for some reason I trusted her. She seems friendlier than her mate.

Slowly I opened my bag and took out the dress. When I held it up for her to look at it she gasped and took a step forward. "That's a really pretty dress..." She said lowly as she stared at the dress. Quickly she shook her head, to get out from the trans.

"Jim said that you hit him with something made out of silver?" She said. I nodded, the tiara.

"Can you show me what you hit him with?" She asked. Without answering her, I showed her the tiara. Her eyes widened, "A tiara?" She asked. I nodded as an answer.

"But you're a werewolf too, how can you touch it?" She asked me. I gave her a weak smile and put on the tiara, to show how it was a perfect fit to my head. Her eyes widened once again and she bowed in front of me, realizing that Im a princess.

When she lifted her head to look at me she smiled, "Can I, can I touch it?" She asked me as she took a step closer to me.

"Sure." I said and lifted the tiara off of my head, so she could touch it. Her hand touched the tiara. She didn't get hurt by the silver, but her hand turned red and she screamed in pain. So witches can't touch it either? What is this?

After she had recovered from the pain a few minutes later she smiled at me. "Come with me, and take that with you." She pointed at the tiara and started walking trough the hallway. I followed her until she stopped outside a living room.

Inside of the room three people sat, a girl who smelled werewolf, a boy who smelled vampire and a human girl. They were all my age.

When me and Cylinda entered the room their heads snapped up towards us. Each one of them bowed their heads, to show their respect for Cylinda, their luna.

"Hello, can you all come over here for a second?" Cylinda asked them. They all stood up from the coach they were sitting in and walked over to us. When they all stood in front of me they looked at me curiously.

"Stella." She turned towards me, telling me to hold up the tiara. I held it up in front of the girls and the boy. They all looked at it with widened eyes.

"Touch it." She said to them. They looked at her and they all frowned, "Why?" The boy asked. His hair was brown, like the girls hair. He was quite tall compared to me and the two girls. His eyes were yellow, but if you looked at them a little bit longer they looked a bit red.

The werewolf girl had long and straight hair down to her collar bones and she had green eyes. She was a little bit taller than me. She looked almost the same as the human girl, besides that the human girl had curly hair and blue eyes. Maybe they are sisters.

"Touch it." Cylinda said, they all looked back at my tiara and then at me. They were all looking at me, head to toe. Then they touched the tiara. They all took away their hands in a matter of a second, screaming in pain.

"What the hell! Is that thing cursed or something!" The curly haired girl said. Cylinda shook her head.

She turned to me, "So you're really a princess?"

Chapter 30

"A princess?" The girls and the boy said in harmony, they all seemed quite shocked by Cylinda's statement. Cylinda nodded. Then she made a gesture towards me.

"She is a princess." She said and then turned towards me. "But I don't know what kind of princess. If she's born in a royal family or not... But she is one."

I shrugged, I don't know either. The only thing I know is that I, in fact, am a princess. Why and how I am one? I have no idea.

"There's many weird things about me..." I said lowly, but unfortunately they all heard. Even the human girl.

"Like what?" She asked. How did she even hear me? Did I really talk that loud? Oh well.

"I can do this..." I said and made all three bow their heads for me. When I let them lift their heads up again they were as shocked as John was when I made him bow.

"Bu-ut you said that there was many things..." The werewolf girl said, stuttering at first but could easily control her voice to sound normal again. She crossed her arms over her stomach and stared me in the eyes.

"Hm, my wolfs color. The fact that I can't see the color of my wolfs eyes. How I got to know that I was a princess. My age when I first shifted. Do I have to keep going?" At the end I was leaning against the doorframe, looking at the teenagers in front of me.

"Tell us everything." Cylinda said. I nodded and walked to the coach and sat down. This is going to take quite some time.

"Where to start?" I asked when everyone was sitting down. The two girls shrugged and leaned back, waiting for me to start. The guy opened his mouth, as he was about to say something when Cylinda spoke, "From the beginning, at the oldest memory of yours."

I nodded slowly, trying to remember everything that happened that night.

Looking down at my hands I started speaking, "When I was about a year old I was found in the forest... I remember almost everything, in detail, from that night..." I started slowly. Without looking up to check if they were listening I carried on with the story.

"I remember being very cold, I was only wrapped in a thin blanket. I was looking up at the sky, no trees or anything was covering it up. The stars were shining as usual, and the moon. It was a bright moon that night, it lit up the forest." I said, imagining that same moon in my head and how it was so bright I could see shadows from the trees. I could see some colors, but not all.

"Then it got dark, something was covering the light up." I frowned at my hands, "It wasn't something, though. It was someone. A wolf, but bigger than a wolf. Then I heard noises, and more of them came out from the bushes around me. There were now eight wolves surrounding me. But I wasn't scared, no, I felt safe." I exhaled. It was dead silent in the room, and everybody was staring at me.

"Suddenly, all the wolves turned into men and women. They were naked, but they had clothes with them, which they put on." I let out a little laugh.

"There were five men and three women. A woman picked me up, and I felt warmth all over my body. She was warming me with her body temperature. She started to talk to me, she said 'Who could have left you here?' Or something like that." I paused and looked up from my hands. Staring at the wall in front of me.

"Another woman, and a man, started arguing. They argued about what they would do with me. The woman didn't want to take me from the woods, the man told her to calm down. I remember hearing the woman who held me saying that I would've got hypothermia and died if they would not take me with them." I sighed, relieved that they took me with them that day.

"Then they ran, really fast. We were soon at their pack house. Then I fell asleep..." I finished.

The human girl was staring at me, her eyes were watering. I could see a tear running down her cheek. The room remained silent for a couple of minutes.

"Do you want to hear more about my life or-"

"Yes!" The girls said, not perfectly synced but enough to make it sound pretty funny.

"I can tell you... About... My best friend?" It came out as a question, but I didn't really know what to tell them about.

They nodded, so I started telling them about Madeleine.

"My best friend, Madeleine, was found in the forest as well, but when she was three years old. She was found just about a week after me. When she got to know that they found another little girl in the forest, just a week ago, she wanted to see me." I smiled at the memory of her three year old face. The stories about her being with Willow so much, just to be near me, were so cute.

"I can't remember so much more from when I was that little, but recently I've been having these weird flashback dreams - and she's in them all..." I said and licked my lips. Then I looked at Cylinda.

"There's a lot more about her." I began and looked over at a painting on the wall.

"She was adopted by the alpha and his mate, only to find out several years later that she actually is a alphas daughter. The alphas son... And my mate, or should I say rejected mate-" The werewolf girl cut me off when I started to talk about Theo.

"Rejected?" She sounded upset, like it was something offensive that I had said to her.

I nodded slowly, "I rejected him." I told her, to clear things up. She got even more upset, but every werewolf, especially she-wolves, gets like this when you talk about rejection.

"Why did you reject him?" She asked before I could say anything else.

"Before you go over to his side, you should here what I think about this. You might think that this is quite a silly cause for me to reject him, but don't judge me." She nodded, understanding my seriousness.

"I've never liked him. Really. Me and Madeleine made songs about how much we hated him and how annoying he was, we often had conversations on how irritating he was." I took a deep breath.

"And, when I was thirteen, on her fifteenth birthday party, he threw a glass of soda on me. I got so angry that I ran home, packed my bags and stole my big brothers motorbike and drove away. I didn't come back until last week... And after being there for almost four days I got banned..." I looked up at the werewolf girl. She didn't look as annoyed anymore.

"Why did you get banned?" She asked softly. I gave her a weak smile.

"His dad, the alpha, got so angry. It was scary, he turned red and his mate couldn't even calm him down. When he found out that I was the one who rejected his son, he kicked me out without even blinking. And worst of all, the ones I called family didn't even care. They just looked at me, they weren't even sad." I said lowly, I didn't realize that a little tear ran down my cheek until it dropped down on my hands.

"And what did you do then? When you were banned?" The guy spoke carefully, as if I was going to burst out in tears if he said it in any other way.

"I took my bags, which I didn't unpack when I got there, and drove away on the motorbike until I was out of gas, in the middle of the forest." I said casually. It wasn't really a big deal for me, driving away from what I used to call home.

I wonder what Madeleine feels like, she must be devastated. I heard that she stopped eating for a while when I was gone the last time. But what will she do now, when she know that I wont come back?

Chapter 31

"**B**ut what about the princess part, how did you get that and the dress?" Cylinda asked and pointed at the tiara which laid beside me in the coach. I picked it up and put it on my head, it was still a perfect fit. The tiara almost felt nice to have on, no scratch that. It felt super nice on my head. I almost don't want to take it off.

"When I woke up two days ago I had never shown anybody my wolf. Later that day, a guy and his friends was going to go for a run and I was going to join them. When we had walked into the forest, I shifted. They were astonished by my wolf. When I went to change back, everything became white. A woman appeared, but everything was white and super blurry. I could see that she was very beautiful. Her voice was as smooth as honey as she spoke. When I woke up I had the dress and the tiara on me. Everyone was really worried, I didn't know why. They told me that I was lifted up in a light beam and then fell down, from several meters up in the air. Then I passed out again. My wolf kept telling me that I was a princess and everybody I walked past in the dress and tiara bowed their heads for me." I told them.

Everybody around me had eyes the size of golfballs, they were really shocked.

"Tell us about your wolf." Cylinda said, she was really curious about me.

"When I went to sleep the night of my seventh birthday everything didn't feel alright. I went out into the forest behind my house, because I knew it would calm me down. Suddenly, I felt a pain shooting trough my spine. I didn't know what was happening, I was really confused. In the matter of some minutes I was standing on four gigantic paws, not on two feet. I rushed to the lake, which I knew was located a few hundred meters into the forest. I didn't see my own reflection in the water, I saw a gigantic wolf." I told them. The reflection of my wolf, of Luceat, in the water was a memory which still was crystal clear.

"I heard a voice in my head, she said 'Don't be afraid, I know that we shouldn't have shifted until we were about thirteen, but we did it now. I am Luceat, your wolf. We can talk inside of our head, it's like mind-linking' Then she told me how to shift back, and so I did. I ran back to my house and put on clothes and then fell asleep. I didn't tell anyone what happened that night, and when I grew older everybody in school called me human. They were not bullying me, just saying that I was a human because 'I hadn't shifted yet' but I didn't want to show anybody my wolf." I said and but my lip.

"Why didn't you want to show it to anybody?" The werewolf girl asked me.

"Because of its color." I said they all frowned. I sighed, I don't want them to ask about the color.

"You can see it. You wont believe me if I say how it looks." I said and they nodded. I looked at the room, there wasn't much space in here.

"But then we need to go to a bigger room." I said and they all nodded and started to walk to another room.

Left, forward, right, right and trough a door. We were in the gym. There were some guys in here, trying to get their six packs to become eight packs or something like that.

Thats when I got an idea. And evil smirk grew on my lips. "Hey!" I called the guys, their heads snapped towards me and I got some confusing looks from Cylinda and the others.

"Does anyone want to fight?" I asked them, they all nodded "In wolf form." I added, they all were still nodding.

"What are you doing? They are the strongest men in our pack!" The vampire dude whispered in my ear. I smirked at him and went into the changing room for girls, it was easy to find. There was a sign hanging over a door.

When I got into the room nobody was in there. I found some training clothes in a basket and put on some shorts and a sports bra. The tiara I left with my clothes.

When I walked out I saw the guys standing in an open space and I walked over there.

"Are your wolves big?" I asked them, they all nodded and held their hands up in the air marking how tall their wolf was. Everyones was shorter than mine, by many centimeters.

"Before we start, please don't cry when I beat you up, okay?" They all laughed as if I was joking, but I was not. I gave them an evil smirk.

They all shifted, two of them had brown wolves, one was grey and the two last ones were darker colors. They were all quite big, but not compared to me.

"Please don't drop your jaws when I shift." I said to them all. The wolves nodded as good as they could and the ones in human form did as well.

Then I did it, I shifted. The familiar sound of bones cracking filled my ears as I felt my blue fur grow out all over me.

Everyone gasped, besides me. I rolled my eyes at them all and had the biggest wolf down on his back before he could blink.

I jumped onto another quite big wolfs back and pushed him down on the floor as well.

The third guy reacted when I was about to jump onto him, and he jumped onto me instead. But he hadn't planned what to do next and didn't expect me rolling onto my back, crushing him against the floor.

I rolled up at my paws and walked towards the two remaining wolves. They were confused and surprised. They were probably thinking things like "how can such a small girl have such a big wolf?"

I could tell that they were a bit more focused on what was happening. They both made the mistake to jump at me, one from the left and one from the right. You don't even need a brain to duck and let them both jump into each other.

When all of the wolves, besides me, was laying down on the floor Cylinda and the teenagers my age cheered. I wonder what their names are, they know mine but I don't know theirs.

I let my tongue hang out of my mouth as I walked to them. They all looked at my wolf in astonishment.

"Wow." The vampire guy said. I took a step forward and raised my head proudly. The werewolf girl laughed.

"Look, the eyes!" He said and everybody looked into my eyes. "Move." He said, and so I did. Right after that I heard gasps.

"Stella, don't shift back. Can we go out for a minute?" Cylinda asked.

It got me confused. Why would we go out? Is there something wrong?

Chapter 32

Although the thought of something being wrong laying in the back of my head, I followed them out. Filling my head with positive thoughts helped a bit to not turn around and walk back. The negative thoughts were not active right now. I had pushed them far back in my head, and focused on the positive ones as I walked. Cylinda opened the door and made a gesture for us all to go out.

When they all stood in front of me they looked up at the sky and then down at my eyes. They didn't talk, however they exchanged some looks with each other before Cylinda spoke.

"Can you move a little bit to the right?" Cylinda asked, to my relieve she didn't sound worried. I moved to the right, as she told me to. They all looked up at the sky once again and down at my eyes.

"Stella, I know - we know - why you don't know what eye color your wolf has." She spoke softly, and slow. Them she walked up to me and let her hands go through my blue fur. I purred in enjoyment, but then looked up at her questioning her. How did they see it? And how couldn't I?

"They are the same color as the sky, and they have stars in them. The stars above you, and me." Cylinda explained.

And then it all came to me, everything.

What those people said, the people who rescued me. I remember it, they told me about it so often. I could heard their voices in my head, "When we rescued you, your eyes were not brown. They were the same color as the sky above you. They also had the stars in them, they moved you moved. The stars were the same as the ones above you, but the moon couldn't be seen in them."

They were spreading rumors, about my eyes. They were only like that that night. Nobody saw my eyes like that after that night. All of them, all eight, were shocked when they saw my eyes in the morning. They were not the same dark blue as the night before, they were dark brown. At least that was what they told me.

"But if her wolfs eyes are reflections of the night sky above her, how do they look in the day?" The vampire boy asked both Cylinda and me. Questioning Cylinda more than me, because I wasn't able to speak in wolf form.

I was as confused with the eyes on the day, I always told myself that I couldn't see them. But no, they were just like the sky above me. Just like at night, but with the day in my eyes.

Cylinda shrugged, she had no idea of what they could look like in the day. "We'll have to wait and see." Cylinda said, she didn't know that I already knew the answer. Or she meant that they would've to wait and then see what I had to say after I shifted back?

The human girl was about to say something, but she got stopped by a blood curdling scream that cut through the air. It came from inside, from the gym.

We were all quick to get in again, to see what had happened inside just seconds ago. There was a new scent in the air, one that wasn't from the guys who I previously beat up. No, this didn't smell like them, it smelled different.

I followed the scent, which lead me into the girls changing room. On the floor was a girl, not much younger that myself. She was screaming and cursing. Her hands she held tight to her chest, as if they were in pain.

I sniffed the air, she was a werewolf. Next to her on the floor was my tiara. She probably was about to go to the gym when she saw it and thought it was pretty, and touched it.

Even though I still was in the form of my blue wolf, I walked up to her. When she noticed me, only seconds later, her eyes widened. Her breath wasn't as calm anymore, and I could hear her heart pounding.

"Calm down Eris." Cylinda said, "She isn't going to hurt you."

The girl named Eris took a quick look at me, but then looking back at her luna. "She?" Eris said, she was surprised. And I wouldn't judge her for that, my wolf isn't the typical she-wolf. It is more masculine, and bigger than a she-wolf would be.

I walked over to the basket with clothes and picked up a t-shirt and a pair of shorts. Then I went into a corner and shifted back, putting on the clothes the second after I was on my two feet.

"Hm." Eris mumbled. She looked a bit like Cylinda, but not enough alike for them to be sisters. They both had orange hair, and were quite pale.

"So, Eris?" I asked, wondering if that was her real name or a nickname of hers. She nodded her head, confirming that Eris is her. I walked up to her and started to talk again, "What made you scream?" I asked her, it was obvious that she had touched the tiara and the burning sensation was to much for her to handle.

And as I thought about it, she turned her head to the side and looked at the tiara. It was still laying on the bench I left it on and the clothes was right beside it. She let out a shaky breath before talking, "That, that thing... It-it..." She stuttered, not able to control her voice.

"Is made out of some material which nobody can touch because it is so weird." I filled in and sat down on the bench, looking down at her. She was still laying on the floor and holding her hands to her chest, tightly.

"How?" She asked, probably wondering how I could've known that. I grinned and looked over at the ones I spent the day with. Even though this is a girl changing room the vampire boy had followed us in, and was standing slightly behind the human girl.

"Are you good at keeping secrets?" I asked her, making her frown in confusion. I asked again, "Are you?"

She nodded slowly, "Yes." Slowly I picked up the tiara and placed it on my head. She gasped and stared at me. I winked at her and giggled.

"Do your hands still hurt?" I asked her. She nodded and looked at her red hands. They did not only look bad, but they smelled bad. The smell of burnt flesh was all over the room, and it was horrible.

"Give me your hands." I said to her, wanting to take a look at them. At first she denied, but then she reached her hands out to me. I grabbed her wrists and the redness faded away swiftly from her hands. Shocked, I frowned down at her hands, as everybody else in the room.

"What the hell just happened?" I whispered to myself.

Her hands just turned normal.

Chapter 33

S he gasped, as the others in the room. We were all stunned by what just happened to her hands, when they touched mine. That wasn't supposed to happen, that can't happen. It's physically impossible! They should be as read and smell as bad as before, and she should go to a doctor. But no, her hands were perfectly fine.

I squeezed and turned her hands repetitively, but she wasn't hurt. Not at all. But she must have been hurt just seconds ago because the smell of burnt flesh was still circling around in the air around us. I looked her in the eyes, "Do they feel ... Normal?" I asked, hoping that she would say no and that my eyes just tricked me and made her hands look normal. We were all waiting for her answer, and to say that my stomach didn't feel good when she nodded was an understatement. It felt like it had twisted itself and then tried to merge out from my skin.

"We need to get you to a doctor, Eris. Even though your hands might feel well, they don't smell good at all. We'll take you to the pack doctor and he'll have a look on them." Cylinda said, making us all nod. Me and the vampire boy - who I still don't know the name of

- helped Eris up and let her lean against us on the way. Even though her hands felt normal, she hadn't recovered from the pain.

"Why did you touch it?" I asked Eris as we walked trough the corridor. My curiousness was to big to calm down, so I had to ask before I went mad.

She sighed, "I just wanted to pick it up, to see the details of it. It was so pretty, I couldn't keep my hands off it." It sure is pretty, with those white gemstones and the silver metal. When I first saw it I was stunned, it isn't just some plastic piece of junk - it is real metal and gems. Where it came from was unclear, I hope nobody stole it to put it on my head while I was unconscious.

"Here we go." Cylinda said when we had walked over a little road, to another house. She was holding up the door for us to come in. Me and the boy let Eris go in herself because we all wouldn't fit in the doorway. Fortunately, she did it well without falling or looking like it was painful to her. She must be recovering from the pain right now, making it easier for her to do stuff without it hurting her.

Cylinda stared into the air for a couple of seconds, she was probably mind-linking the doctor to come here and take a look at Eris hands. And I was right, shortly a man came rushing from the corridor. He bowed his head in respect for the Luna and then looked at everybody else.

"So, who is hurt?" He asked us all. We all looked over at Eris who gave the doctor a weak smile. She wasn't proud of being hurt, but who would? He looked her over and then frowned, "Where are you hurt?" He asked as he could not see anything bleeding or any places on her that looked hurt.

Eris hold up her hands, making the doctor frown even more. He walked up to her and took her wrists in his hands, looking at her hands, just as I did minutes ago. Then he looked at Cylinda, still frowning. He didn't understand anything. Maybe he thought that this was some kind of prank we were pulling on him. He let go of Eris' wrists and walked up to his Luna. His faces showed nothing else than confusion when he spoke, "I can't see anything wrong with her hands."

"I'll let her explain." Cylinda said and turned towards me. The doctor did the same. He looked at me and then at the tiara which was placed on my head, just for a second. He walked up to me, giving me a questioning look, wanting me to explain.

I could either do it the boring way, or the fun way. And as the person I am, I'll choose the fun way.

"Touch it." I said and took the tiara off my head. He looked at me and then at it, skeptical. He didn't know how to act, else than touch the tiara. And so he did. When his hand landed on the beautiful silver ring he squealed in pain, drawing everybody in the waiting rooms attention. He excused himself as he was holding his hand.

I put on the tiara again, and it felt as nice as before.

"Give me your hands." I said, looking at the man. He frowned and looked up at me, meeting my serious eyes. I tried to look as serious as possible, and to my relieve I succeed.

"Why?" He asked, not wanting to give me his hands.

"Trust me, give me your hands." I said, almost demanding him to do it. He reached his hands out to me. The right one was all read and had the horrible smell of burnt flesh radiating from it. So he was right handed. Not really the greatest information, but you never know when you can use it.

I took his wrist in my hand, the same way I did with Eris' hands. And as I expected, his hand turned normal. He was shocked, he almost choked on his own breath. His eyes was widened, I expected nothing less. Everybody had widened eyes when I spoke to them about the princess thing, or did this. But I have only done this two times now.

"H-ow did y-you?" He asked, backing away from me a bit. His way of talking and from the way he acted drew many peoples attention. They were probably curious of what happened, and I wont blame them. I would be curious too.

I shook my head, "I don't know." He frowned at me, as if he thought that I was lying. He didn't trust me, nor my words. As he was staring down at his hand I took some time to look him up and down. He has dark brown hair and as usual, he is muscular. His outfit was a black t-shirt, a pair of dark jeans and a white coat that screamed doctor from long way. If I was correct, I would say that he is about 26 years old and has probably not found his mate yet.

"Liar. If you knew how to do it, then you know how." He said cockily when he had got some courage. I growled loudly, making him almost jump back. I glared at him, "Now I wish that I wouldn't have healed your hands." I said lowly and took a step forward.

He growled back, even higher, "Don't step closer, kid." He said cockily, once again. His attitude is definitely going on my nerves. But instead of coming up with a great comeback I laughed a little and grinned. He looked weirdly at me, as if I was crazy.

"I wouldn't say so if I was you, Patrick." Cylinda chuckled. He frowned at her and then looked at her the same way as he recently looked at me, "And why shouldn't I? She's just a kid!"

Me, Cylinda and the three teenagers laughed, making him even more confused. "She's a higher rank that you, Pat." Cylinda said when she had stopped laughing. Patrick furrowed his eyebrows at her.

"What? But I'm Beta, she can't be a higher rank than me. She's just a kid!" He claimed. That got me wondering, why did the Beta work as a pack doctor? Maybe he's just a stand in for someone?

"She is." Cylinda said calmly. But that was the opposite of what Patrick was right now, he was everything besides calm. He was confused, angry, and even more confused.

"Is she an Alpha's daughter?" He asked after he had been thinking for a while. Cylinda shook her head and gave him a goofy smile. He however didn't return one, he found this situation weird. And I? I don't know, I was just standing there and listening to their conversation.

"Higher rank." Cylinda said, still with that same goofy smile on her lips.

"She can't be an Alpha, nor a Luna. She is too young." He said, thinking. I could tell he was thinking hard, he couldn't figure a thing out though.

"Still, higher rank." Cylinda said. Her smile had turned into a playful one and I could tell that she found this situation hilarious.

"She can't be a higher rank." Patrick stated, but he was wrong. We all shook our heads. He was still confused, really confused.

"What do you think this is?" I asked him after taking off the tiara once again. He looked over at me and shrugged.

"A silve- How the hell can you hold that thing?" He asked in panic. His eyes widened once again.

"I am the only one who can hold this, or even touch it." I told him and put it on again. I gave him a little playful smile and leaned forward to his ear and whispered, "Can you guess what I am now?"

Chapter 34

I slowly pulled back from whispering in his ear. Shocked was an understatement, he looked more than shocked. If that even was possible. He frowned and scratched his neck, thinking. When he stopped scratching it looked like a light bulb popped up over his head, in my imagination I could see one. And the light was making me want to blink and look another way.

"A p-pri-" He stuttered, but we cut him off, all five. We shook our heads at him, telling him to keep silent about it. When we stopped shaking our heads he nodded, understanding that he must be keeping his mouth shut about this.

"Why are you here on our territory?" Patrick asked me in confusion. I gave him a weak smile and let Cylinda answer, "She joined our pack yesterday."

"But why can't I mind-link her then?" He asked, Cylinda just stared at him. She was a Luna, but she was still a witch. I am unsure if she can mind-link with anyone in the pack or not, being their Luna.

"I can't mind-link you either..." The werewolf girl said to me, confused to why this was happening. So I forgot to tell them about the mind-link thing? Guess I have to explain it to them now.

"Err, so, uh. My best friend Madeleine is the only one who can mind-link me ... And ... A guy ..." I said, unsure if I wanted to tell them about him. They all nodded slightly and looked at me. We were still drawing attention from the people in the waiting room, but I didn't really care. They would figure out eventually.

"So, are her hands - and your - fine?" I asked, coming back to what we were here to do. Eris hands didn't smell horrible anymore, but Patrick's hand had left a smell of burnt flesh in the air, which wouldn't go away.

"Yeah, you can go." He said and we all nodded and walked out of the building. Eris thanked me for making her hands feel good again and gave me a hug, of course I hugged back.

"Thank you, thank you, thank you!" She said happily when she released me from the hug. She had a big bright smile on her lips as she spoke to me. I smiled back at her, to be nice and because I liked this girl.

"I have to go home now and eat dinner. I'll see you at school?" She asked me. I shrugged, I hadn't thought about school yet, to be honest I haven't thought about nearly anything besides getting a pack or somewhere to stay. Eris furrowed her eyebrows, "You are going to school, right?" She asked in confusion. I shrugged again, I really didn't know.

"Don't know. I mean, I would-"

"Yes, yes she is going to school." Cylinda cut me off. Eris smiled and then waved at us before leaving. I watched her run to a couple of houses before she was just a little dot. Then I turned around, facing Cylinda with a raised eyebrow.

"I will talk to the principal." She said, and I nodded. We all started walking back to the pack house, which I thought was a bit weird. Didn't they have houses to go to? Cylinda should at least go to the Alpha's house, where she probably lives with her mate.

When we were getting closer to the pack house I could see something standing in front of it. I looked at it, trying to see what it was. And then I saw it.

"My motorbike!" I squealed and ran up to my bike. To my luck, my helmet was on the ground next to my motorbike. The bike was cleaned and filled up with gas. I clapped my hands and was as excited as a kid on Christmas.

"Is that yours?" Someone asked from behind me. I turned around and almost bumped into the vampire guy. Slowly I nodded, "Yeah."

"Really?" He said, raising his eyebrows. He sounded like he didn't believe me. I could see that he liked my motorbike, by the way he looked at it. In his eyes was jealousy, and he looked like he wanted to marry it. But unfortunately, it's mine. And I am the one who's marrying it, if someone would.

"Yeah, I stole it from my brother when I was thirteen." I said, remembering that I told him about me stealing Travis' motorcycle and getting it from him when I got back.

"Hm." He muttered and I could see his eyes turn a little more yellow, even though it was almost pitch black. I have no idea what day, or what time, it is. All I knew is that it is the end of the summer, and that the leaves of the trees are slowly turning other colors. But they are not falling down yet. I would guess that it is late August or early September.

"Should we go in or not?" The human girl asked. She had goosebumps all over her arms. I nodded, walking inside of the house with her. The aroma of chicken filled my nostrils and Luceat purred, we love chicken. I could see the werewolf girl sniffing the air too, her eyes turned darker. She turned her head towards me, smirking. I returned a smirk and we both started running towards the chicken.

I came into the room where they ate before the girl, but she joined my side in a matter of seconds. "Dang, your fast!" She said and I gave her a smile.

The others joined us about a minute later, talking about something. But I didn't listen. I wanted chicken.

As we walked through the big room everybody bowed their heads for their Luna, Cylinda answered them with a nod or smile. This is another reason for me not wanting to be a Luna, you always have to be nice to the pack members. I want to act rude to everybody, especially the ones who I hate.

"Let's sit here." The human girl said and sat down on a chair next to the wall. The table in front of it was big, compared to the ones in my old packs room for eating in. This table fit eight people, the ones at my old packs house only fitted four.

I got to sit next to the vampire boy and an empty chair. In front of me the werewolf girl sat, to her right the human girl sat and to the left Cylinda sat.

"Oh god, we've forgotten to introduce ourselves!" The werewolf girl said as an excuse. I smiled down at the table, she sounded quite silly saying that.

"Anyways, I'm Tessla. Like Tess, but with 'la' at the end." She said. So the werewolf girls name's Tessla. That is a really pretty name, but werewolves usually have unique or really pretty names.

I nodded, confirming that I heard her. Then giving her a smile before the other girl started talking, "And I'm Amber." She said. I gave her a smile and a nod too.

"Cedric." The vampire boy said and I nodded. He was not getting a smile from me, he clearly wants to marry my motorbike and he is not going to do that. Not for as long as I live. And I can tell you, werewolves live long.

Everybody got quiet when a door opened and the alpha came out. I smiled down at my hands when I saw red marks from my tiara all over his face, and on his arms.

Some people gasped when they saw the marks and Cylinda raised her eyebrows and looked over at me. I sucked my lips into my mouth, to keep me from laughing when she looked at me. But she didn't look angry, to my relieve.

"What happened, Alpha?" Someone asked, wondering what the hell had happened to his alpha's face and some bit of his arms.

"A person hit me with a silver thing." He said angrily and growled lowly. As he spoke he made his way over to my table. He stopped right in front of me. People started whispering and gasping once again. Their eyes were locked at me. Some pople looked at me with anger in their eyes, and others with surprise.

Right before he spoke, I made him bow. Just because that would make him look stupid.

Everybody in the room gasped once again, besides me, Tessla, Amber, Cedric and Cylinda who laughed. It surprised me that Cylinda laughed, it was her mate who I was embarrassing.

"Why are you laughing?" He asked his mate. Cylinda smiled widely and shook her head. He mate was getting so angry that he almost turned red.

"How?" He asked me, probably asking how I made him bow. I shrugged.

"She's the witch, not me?" I said, but it sounded more like a question. Cylinda nodded, covering my identity as a princess. I turned my head towards her and mimed, 'Thank you' She responded with a smile.

"I just wanted to have a little fun, alright?" Cylinda said and gave her mate a loving smile, calming him down. He nodded, understandingly but then looked at me. No, glared at me.

"But you still shoved that silver thing up in my face." He was still glaring at me. Fortunately, he didn't know that the tiara was the silver thing.

"Because you ruined my dress." I glared back at him.

"You can buy a new one." He said with a low growl.

"I don't think so." I responded, a dress like that would coast at least a million. And I don't even have a cent.

"Why don't you think so?" He asked me, still glaring at me with hatred in his eyes.

"I don't have any money, and if that dress would've been in a store it would have coasted over a couple of million dollars." I confessed. Lost of people who were overhearing the conversation frowned. I heard some people whisper things like, "How did she buy that?" and "A couple million dollars? Sure." Some people thought I was joking about what it coast. But to me, it was a million dollar gown. Even though that sounds like me picking out a wedding dress, it wasn't. I didn't get to pick this one, yet it fit my body perfectly and had the prettiest color, and gems.

"Pfft." He responded.

"It is covered in gems. Real gems. The. Whole. Freaking. Dress." I said lowly, all werewolves in the room gasped and looked angrily at their alpha.

"And where did you get the money to buy that in the first place?" He asked with a raised eyebrow.

"I didn't buy it ... I got it." I said looking down at the table.

"So what?" He asked. He tilted his head slightly and glared at me.

"She wont be happy ... Whoever she is." I murmured down at my hands. I hope that that woman in white wont kill him or take his wolf from him. I've heard that goddesses can do such things to wolves when they disrespect someone who shouldn't be disrespected. And for as far as I know, princesses should get respected - or consequences. I am pretty sure that the woman I saw that day was a goddess, she was so pretty and her whole body - and her voice - was just screaming goddess.

"I hope she doesn't kill you..." I murmured a bit higher, so he would hear it for sure. And he did. His face turned into a weird expression and he looked shocked at my words.

"What?" He asked me, asking for me to tell him what I was going on about. I just shook my head and made my lips into a thin line.

"What?" Even thought he knew that the alpha tone don't work on me, he used it. I just shook my head once again and looked down at my feet underneath the table.

"You have to obey me, I am your alpha." While he spoke a loud growl escaped him, causing many people to jump back or hid their faces in their mates hair or chest. I, however, didn't do anything but smirk down at my feet.

I shook my head, thinking about what I am. The same smirk was extending on my lips, and I was almost grinning. He growled once again, a bit louder, expecting me to whimper or get scared. But I did not, I was still calm - looking down at my feet with a big grin all over my lips.

"You know what happens then, don't you?" Jim gave me a smirk before speaking again, not only to me but to all the beings in this room, "If you don't respect your alpha, what happens then, Stella?" When he said my name it was like venom was running down from his mouth. Even though he was angry, he hid it with a smirk. He was amused by what was going to happen. I would be locked up in a cell, with silver chains on arms and legs.

"I know what happens," I said calmly, "However, I am not scared of it." Shrugging I looked up at him, meeting a confused face.

"Take her to the cell!" Alpha Jim shouted. Two buff guys stood up, one of them was one of the guy I fought at the gym. He is probably one of the strongest in this pack. To me? No, not really. He was an easy match for me.

The guy from the gym froze when he looked at me, recognizing my face and features. He turned his face to his alpha, "I am not going near her."

"And why is that?" The alpha asked in confusion. A little chuckle escaped me. I heard my company chuckling a little bit too.

"Who is the strongest fighter in this pack?" I asked in pure curiosity. The alpha furrowed his eyebrows at me and turned around, facing the people in the cafeteria.

"Otis!" The alpha spoke and then a buff guy stood up. He wasn't one of those from the gym, but he looked just as strong as them. He walked over to his alpha and then looked down at me.

"Can you shift for me?"

Chapter 35

"Why would I do that?" The buff man, who I assume is Otis, frowned at my question. Obviously it wasn't quite normal for a little girl to ask him to shift.

"Hm, I could just shift and rip your head from your body before you could blink, but I wont." I cocked my head to the side, looking at the muscular man in front of me. I now noticed that he wasn't a man, he was just a little older than me. Maybe about a year and a half.

"I doubt that you could do that." He said, looking me over. My body isn't that muscular, but my wolf is. He on the other side was really muscular, almost looking like an alphas son, but not quite buff enough. Maybe a beta's son.

"You shouldn't doubt her." The man from the gym said loudly, he was a tiny bit afraid. I could tell it by his voice, and something in his eyes.

"Why?" The Otis guy asked and turned around to face the man. He was both curious and confused. I would be too, if I didn't know a single thing about me besides that I had disrespected the alpha.

They looked each other in the eyes, probably mind-linking. Otis'
eyes widened and he gasped, "She did what?"

"Otis, Gerard?" The alpha asked them, "What did he tell you, Otis?"
Jim demanded, he didn't have to use his alpha tone for Otis to answer.

"She beat up five guys just an hour ago in the gym in less than five
minutes." Otis said to his alpha, and to all people in the room. Many
people looked at me, wide-eyed. They didn't believe it, I could tell.

"Sure." The alpha said sarcastically and rolled his eyes. Another
one who doesn't believe what I had done. But that was just playing
around in the gym, I just wanted to see how good their fighters were.

"It's true." Cylinda filled in, Tessla, Amber and Cedric nodded. Jim
looked at his mate in confusion, but she was still nodding.

"You have seen my wolf. I wouldn't doubt it if I was you." I said and
stood up, still shorter than Jim and Otis.

"Lead her to the cell." Jim said to Otis. Otis nodded and took a hold
on my arm, making me growl at him. He bit his lip and looked back
at the man from the gym.

"How big is your wolf?" I asked him, to see how small it is compared
to mine and how easy he will be to take down.

When he wouldn't answer I got frustrated, "Can you at least tell me
your rank then?"

He smirked at me, convinced that he was a higher rank than me. "I
am the son of a beta." He told me and then looked down at me. "And
you're probably an omega."

I laughed, even though we still stood in front of a hundred pack members I thought that we still would be able to have a conversation with him.

"What? What rank are you then?" He asked me. He was curious and confused to why I laughed. I really look like an omega, but I surely am not one.

"Ask your Luna." I said, making Jim growl at me for mentioning his mate, and at Otis for looking at Cylinda. To my relieve, she just shook her head and smiled.

"Go to the cell with her, now!" Jim growled.

Otis looked at his alpha, stood still for a second and then nodded. He started dragging me again, but he was not able to pull me with him.

'Run, run away from this place! They will put us in a cell!' Luceat said, whining. But I wont listen to her, not right now. I don't want to leave all my stuff behind.

"What are you waiting for, go!" Alpha Jim shouted with a loud growl. He pushed my back, so hard I almost fell on the floor.

That. Is. It.

A loud growl escaped my lips and I shifted. Bones cracked and fur grew out. When I looked down again I saw a pair of massive paws.

People were gasping, their jaws were falling off by now. Otis froze beside me.

'Can I force him to shift?' Luceat asked, wanting to see his wolf really bad. Probably because she wanted to fight him.

'Wait, can we force people to shift?' I asked. Luceat laughed and said something sounding like an 'Of course' between the laughs.

Then his eyes widened as he started turning into a wolf. In the matter of a few seconds a black wolf with grey eyes stood in front of me. It was smaller than me, but not as small as the guys I fought at the gym. Probably because he is the son of a beta, they are usually larger.

I jumped onto his back, making him fall down at the floor. Then I stood up an pressed one of my front paws on his throat and the other one on his belly. I growled at the alpha who had widened eyes, as the others in the room. The only calm ones was that guy from the gym, Cylinda, Tessla, Amber and Cedric. They were just smiling.

'That was soooooooooo easy!' Luceat said, but she wasn't unhappy. She just threw their best fighter to the ground in a couple of seconds.

"And once again, he didn't listen to me." The guy from the gym muttered and poked with his fork in the food that had been served while we were arguing.

Otis didn't move underneath me, he knew that if he did a wrong move, he could accidentally break his neck and die. Instead he just whined, wanting me to step away from him.

I stepped off of Otis and walked back to my new friends. Jim growled loudly, because I was next to his mate. The growl didn't scare me, Cylinda wouldn't let him hurt me nor me hurt him. I put my head on Tessla's lap and let her pet my head. Shutting my eyes for a minute was calming. It felt like I could fall asleep at any moment if she carried on.

My eyes snapped open when I heard a growl from behind me. I turned around and saw Jim's wolf. It looked just as it did that one day in the forest one and a half day ago.

His wolf was smaller than mine, but not as much as all other wolves in this pack. He was the alpha of the pack, making him bigger than everyone else. Besides me.

I tilted my big head to the side, looking at him. He growled once again and showed me his canines. I was standing still, but he moved closer and closer to me. Another growl escaped him, wanting me to get away from his mate.

Cylinda was sitting next to the wall, and next to Tessla. That made me standing next to her.

Jim growled loudly, making many people in the room back away from this part of the big room. They are expecting a fight. However, I don't want to fight him in front of Cylinda. She would be mad at me if I hurt him.

I growled lowly, not wanting him to come any where near me. Even though he didn't want me to be near his mate, I knew that she was scared. Jim was probably too angry to realize it. But I was going to protect her and my new friends if he would attack.

He growled again and took a step towards us. I took a step to the side, making him unable to get to Cylinda. I could hear her heart beat really fast.

I am angry, at him. But not only at him, I am angry at many people. But Jim is definitely number one, right now.

Suddenly, he was lying on the floor whimpering. He looked at me, his heart was beating faster than Cylinda's.

What? Did Cylinda do that?

'No, dumb ass. You did!' Luceat said and rolled her eyes at my stupidity. But how? How was I able to do that?

'You're a princess, remember?' Luceat explained. So I had powers as a princess? Luceat nodded.

Then, it stopped. He wasn't whimpering anymore, he was standing up looking directly at Cylinda.

A shirt was thrown at me, I caught it in my mouth. I turned around and shifted. The second I was back at my two feet, I put the shirt on making sure nobody saw my naked body.

When I turned around once again, Jim stood there in a pair of shorts. He started walking to his mate, but I walked out in the way of him, stopping him from reaching her.

"What are you doing?" He asked angrily and tried to shove me away. It didn't work though, he's too weak to do that.

"You're scaring her!" I said and received a growl from him. He walked past me and up to a frightened Cylinda. Her heart beat raised, making me confused. Was that even possible?

Then something happened, something I thought would never ever happen.

Chapter 36

Tessla growled at Jim. She growled at her alpha. She stepped in front of him, covering Cylinda with her back.

Jim looked shocked, and angry. "Get. Out. My. Way!" He growled at her. Tessla was shaking her head. I have no clue why she just did that. Does she want to get locked in a cell?

"I am your alpha, you need to obey me!" He growled and glared at Tessla. Tessla was scared, her heart was beating a little bit faster than normal, but she stayed calm.

"I am just protecting my Luna." Tessla said and let out a shaky breath. Then she took a quick looka at me, before looking back at her alpha.

"Protecting her of what?" The alpha asked, he wanted to be with his mate. Unfortunately, he is stupid and doesn't get that Cylinda is hyperventilating behind Tessla.

"Something that scares the shit out of her right now." Tessla said coldly and glared at Jim before adding a word, "No, excuse me. Someone." She corrected herself and glared at her alpha.

"Who?" He asked. Oh god, how stupid can you be?

"You." I said coldly from his behind.

"Wh-what... N-no!" Jim said stuttering, he looked sad. It was almost making me sad too. Almost.

I sighed and put my hand on my head. The bun was still there. And the tiara ... Weird. Maybe tiaras doesn't break while shifting? I honestly have no idea, I've never tried before.

"She is clearly really afraid right now, and when you're stepping closer her heart beat raises." Cedric said, he then looked like he gave himself a mental face palm.

Tessla and Amber nodded in agreement, so did I. It was true, Cylinda got scared by her mate right now. And because she isn't a werewolf she doesn't feel the mate pull as much either.

"And when I think about it, she's not the only one who's scared of you right now." I said and folded out my arm in the direction of the pack members on the other side of the room. All stood very close to the wall. Mates were holding each other and kids had their hands in their ears and their eyes shut.

The alpha growled loudly at me, "Get her to the cell, now!" He said agrily in his alpha tone.

Otis, who still was laying on the ground, stood up and walked to me and dragged me through the room.

"Don't let him near her!" I shouted before we left the room, hoping that they would listen to me. Cylinda should not be near Jim until she isn't scared anymore.

"Okay ... Can your answer some questions for me?" Otis asked when he dragged me through the corridor. I shrugged, but then nodded at him. He can get the answers he want, but I am not promising to tell him the truth.

"How can you look like an omega when your wolf is ... Well, humongous?" He asked me while dragging me around a corner.

"That's something I don't want to tell you." I said as a response. It was true, he would tell everything to the alpha. And I want the alpha to know less than he already knew.

"Hm ... Okay then ... How do you know the Luna?" He asked curiously and looked at me for once.

"After I had ... Hurt the alpha ... Cylinda came to my room and then we walked to the living room and me, her, Tessla, Amber and Cedric talked for a while. Then we went to the gym, because they wouldn't believe me if I told them what color my wolf is. And then I ... Helped a girl and the Beta with ... Some things ..." I told him, leaving some holes in my sentences, not wanting him to know those things. And I am not filling in those holes anywhere soon.

"Mhm ..." He murmured and then before saying anything else he stopped, making me bump in to his back.

I front of us was a metal door, which Otis knocked on. "Name and rank!" A dark voice said from the other side of the door.

"Otis Jones, Warrior." Then the door opened, revealing loads of cells with silver colored metal bars. They were probably silver too.

"A girl?" The same voice said, the man who it belonged to sat on a chair with a desk in front of him.

"Yeah." Otis said and smirked.

"So, what is her name, rank and why is she here?" The man asked.

Otis looked down at me, wanting me to tell him all of that information.

"Uh, Stella Adams, I'd rather not tell anyone here my rank and I am here because the alpha destroyed my dress." I said and gave him a fake smile, making sure it looked fake too.

"Just because he destroyed your dress?" The man asked, frowning at me.

"No, I was protecting the Luna too." I said, because that was true. I protected her from being scared as hell and uncomfortable.

"Err... Okay..." The man said sounding really confused, but he still wrote it down.

"Fill this in, please." He said and gave me a bunt of paper with text on it. The he gestured for me to sit down in front of him. I did so and picked up a pen.

Gender: Female.

Full name: Stella Adams.

Eye-color: Brown.

Hair-color: Brown.

Height: 174 cm. (5'8")

Weight: You should never ask a woman that question...

I was happy with my answers. I didn't answer many of the other questions, just a few.

When I handed the papers to the man he smiled at me, not with a friendly smile though.

"Lead her to cell A67." The man said, not looking up from the papers. Otis gasped, was it really that bad of a cell?

Otis lead me through the corridor of cells. In every other cell there was a man or woman. Most of them were frightening and had many scars.

Otis stopped at the last door. It was a door, not a cell.

He opened the door carefully and stepped in. I did so too. In there was a chair, a silver chair with silver hand cuffs on it.

'I told you to run! We would've been safe if we had ran away!' Luceat complained.

"Sit down." Otis said. My legs felt wobbly while walking to the middle of the room. I sat down in the chair, expecting it to hurt me more than anything. But to my surprise - nothing. My bum just felt a little bit cold.

I looked up at Otis, meeting his gaze. His eyes showed pure confusion, and something else. He looked ... Scared?

"H-how?" Otis stuttered. I smirked at him, so I was immune to silver?

Chapter 37

Theo's POV

I was walking around my room, in wolf form. I had been in wolf form for three days now - ever since Stella got banned. For all that I know in this world, I will not forgive my father. Not today, not tomorrow, never.

Not leaving my room was hard, I had nothing to do besides being sad. The though of the possibility of never seeing my mate again made my chest hurt. I couldn't stand the pain very good.

I haven't gone to school since Sunday. All I have been doing is walking around in my room, sleeping and howling. Howls was the only thing I let out of myself, besides tears and whimpers.

A knock on the door got my attention, "Theo, you need to get out of there!" It was my mom. She was really worried about me. I liked that about her, that she cares about me. But it is my dad who's the problem here, not her. I wont let anyone from the pack in here, everyone will tell my dad about what they have seen and what I have said to them.

The knocks disappeared after a little while, then I heard footsteps walking away from my room. They already knew that the door was locked.

Maybe I need to get out of here? I would like to run in the forest for a little while.

'Me too.' My wolf Geo said, thinking about the forest surrounding the little village our pack lived in.

I shifted back to human form. It felt weird to stand on two feet again, to have hands and feet instead of paws. Even though I am mostly human, it felt strange to be in this form. I've never been in wolf form that long, the longest I had been a wolf for was about five hours. But now it was three days.

I put on a pair of black basketball shorts and a white t-shirt before leaving the room. It felt strange to walk, but at the same time it was strangely satisfying.

'I'm going out for a run, wanna come?' I mind-linked Maddie. She also had been locking herself inside of her room, angry at dad and everything really. We had been mind-linking when we were bored, everybody else I shut out. Madeleine was the only person who felt the same pain as me.

'Sure...' Maddie responded quietly and shortly I heard her door open behind me.

We walked down the stairs while looking down at our feet. My mom quickly rushed to us with a worried expression on her face. I probably had dark rings beneath my eyes, just as Maddie had. My eyes were probably red from crying, like hers.

"Where are you two going?" She asked with a worried tone. We didn't answer. I didn't answer because I didn't want to talk. Why Maddie didn't speak I had no clue of. Maybe she was so hurt she couldn't speak without breaking out into tears.

"I'll have to have a serious talk with him..." Mom said angrily to herself and it was obvious that she meant dad. She is going to talk to dad, and tell him what a idiot he is. It made me smile on the inside, my mom is really overprotective with me and Maddie. My dad however has been sitting in his office, doing pack stuff, all week.

I looked up at my mom, she gave me a sad smile and embraced me in a thigh hug. I answered the hug and cried silently into her shoulder. She started petting my head, calming me down a bit.

"Do you want to go to school today? It starts in an hour." Mom said when we pulled out from the hug. I swiped away the tears and nodded. I need to go to school, I can't just stay home all week. Even though I'm sad. Plus that it is unhealthy to just stay in my room all week, I need to get out. And I don't want to get bad grades in school or miss anything important.

I walked into the kitchen and grabbed a peach. Maddie took one too, even though she isn't going to school today she needs to eat. Everybody does.

"I can drive you there." Mom offered. I shook my head, I wanted to walk. Maddie smiled at my mother, a smile that said "don't be worried, he'll do just fine".

When I was done eating the peach I threw the core in the crash can. My steps lead my up to my room. When I went in I went straight to the closet. I put on a pair of socks and a hoodie. I left the hoodie open, it was one of those with a zipper through the middle of it.

My outfit isn't the best, but it is good enough. Even though it's cold outside, I am a werewolf. We are warmer than humans, which makes us able to be naked outside in the middle of the winter without freezing to death.

I ran down the creaking stairs and down to the hall. Choosing shoes was easy, I just had two pairs. I had a pair of black vans and a pair of white training shoes. I put on my vans and my blue backpack, then I started walking to school.

On the ten minute walk I heard the birds chirp a little melody. On a normal day I would hear it as a happy little song, but now it was sad. I tried to make it a happy tune in my head, but it didn't work.

"Hey man!"

I turned around to see my best friend Aden waving furiously at me. He had a big bright smile on his lips as he walked up to me. The school building was just a few meters away from us, I was just about to walk in when he spoke again.

"Where have you been all week?" He asked me and opened the door. So nobody knew what happened that day? This will make my day even harder than I thought.

'Home.' I mind-linked him. He nodded in confusion of why I used the mind-link rather than speak.

When we walked through the corridor everybody moved away so we easily could walk to our lockers.

"Theo!" A high pitched voice said, a voice which belongs to the most annoying girl in this school.

"Where have you been? I was so worried for you!" She obviously has a huge crush on me.

"Katharine, leave him alone." Aden said, and to my relieve she left after giving Aden a glare. I gave him a little smile and got my stuff for the next class.

'If someone asks, I have a sour throat and cannot speak or else I will loose my voice. Alright?' I mind-linked to Aden. He gave me a nod as we entered the classroom. Today I felt like sitting in the back, so we sat down right next to the back wall.

The teacher started the lesson and started talking about some historical stuff, I don't listen much at what he's saying, but I snap up a few things that could be handy to know later when we have tests.

When the lesson is over me and Aden leave quickly. I didn't really want people to ask me where I've been the past days, I didn't really want to answer anyone.

When we walked past some lockers I could smell Stella's scent. Her locker must be near me, I remember seeing her around this part of school with a open locker in front her.

Instantly I looked down at my feet and bit my bottom lip. The thought of never seeing her again popped up in my head. I wanted to cry, but I couldn't. Not when I am in school, and on top of that - all my tears were gone. I had cried so much these past days and therefor none was left.

Aden nudged my arm, 'What is it?'

'Nothing.' I answered.

'I can see that you're sad, why?' Aden asked as he stopped walking, making me stand still too.

'Theo?' Aden said strictly, wanting me to explain the situation.

'Dad found out who my mate was...' I said slowly. He nodded understandingly and waited for me to explain more.

'He banned her from our territory...' I said lowly. Thank god that we have this mind-link, I wouldn't want any other person to know this. Aden gasped and widened his eyes, understanding why I had been home all week.

'I felt that something was wrong when we were on our little run, so thats why I ran away and why my dad was at those omegas house...' I explained, reminding him of what happened. Al though that was much of the truth, I didn't tell him all of it.

'Was... Was Stella your mate?' I nodded at his words, yes she was.

'So thats why she is gone...' Aden murmured and I nodded once again.

'Please don't tell anyone!' I pleaded. He nodded, confirming that he will not be telling anyone about what happened. Hopefully I can thrust him.

"Hey guys!" My friend Jonathan approached us with a big smile.

"Did you hear about that girl who beat the alpha of the Unwanted's ass up?" Jonathan said and chuckled. A girl?